Mac hesitated a moment or two before making a grudging admission. "Maybe I was out of line, pushing at you the way I did."

"Maybe?"

"Okay, I tend to come on a little strong at times. The point is, I shouldn't have ragged you. Not about something so important. That isn't the kind of decision a person should make right before taking off on a mission."

The comment took Cari completely aback. After that bone-rattling kiss this afternoon, she would have thought he'd be the last one to suggest she'd make a mistake.

"When did my personal life become a matter of such interest to you?"

"Since the first time I laid eyes on you." He dropped the bombshell so casually that it took a few seconds for the full impact to hit.

"Are you saying you've...you've...?"

"Had the hots for you since day one? As a matter of fact, I have."

Dear Reader,

As always, Silhouette Intimate Moments is coming your way with six fabulously exciting romances this month, starting with bestselling Merline Lovelace, who always has *The Right Stuff.* This month she concludes her latest miniseries, TO PROTECT AND DEFEND, and you'll definitely want to be there for what promises to be a slam-bang finale.

Next, pay another visit to HEARTBREAK CANYON, where award winner Marilyn Pappano knows *One True Thing:* that the love between Cassidy McRae and Jace Barnett is meant to be, despite the lies she's forced to tell. Lyn Stone begins a wonderful new miniseries with *Down to the Wire.* Follow DEA agent Joe Corda to South America, where he falls in love—and so will you, with all the SPECIAL OPS. Brenda Harlen proves that sometimes *Extreme Measures* are the only way to convince your once-and-only love— and the child you never knew!—that this time you're home to stay. When *Darkness Calls,* Caridad Piñeiro's hero comes out to...slay? Not exactly, but he *is* a vampire, and just the kind of bad boy to win the heart of an FBI agent with a taste for danger. Finally, let new author Diana Duncan introduce you to a *Bulletproof Bride,* who quickly comes to realize that her kidnapper is not what he seems—and is a far better match than the fiancé she was just about to marry.

Enjoy them all—and come back next month for more of the best and most exciting romance reading around, right here in Silhouette Intimate Moments.

Yours,

[signature]

Leslie J. Wainger
Executive Editor

Please address questions and book requests to:
Silhouette Reader Service
U.S.: 3010 Walden Ave., P.O. Box 1325, Buffalo, NY 14269
Canadian: P.O. Box 609, Fort Erie, Ont. L2A 5X3

MERLINE LOVELACE
The Right Stuff

Silhouette®

INTIMATE MOMENTS™

Published by Silhouette Books

America's Publisher of Contemporary Romance

SILHOUETTE BOOKS

ISBN 0-373-27349-5

THE RIGHT STUFF

Copyright © 2004 by Merline Lovelace

This edition published by arrangement with Harlequin Books S.A.

® and TM are trademarks of Harlequin Books S.A., used under license. Trademarks indicated with ® are registered in the United States Patent and Trademark Office, the Canadian Trade Marks Office and in other countries.

Visit Silhouette at www.eHarlequin.com

Printed in U.S.A.

Books by Merline Lovelace

Silhouette Intimate Moments

Somewhere in Time #593
*Night of the Jaguar #637
*The Cowboy and the
  Cossack #657
*Undercover Man #669
*Perfect Double #692
†The 14th...and Forever #764
Return to Sender #866
**If a Man Answers #878
The Mercenary and the
  New Mom #908
**A Man of His Word #938
Mistaken Identity #987
**The Harder They Fall #999
Special Report #1045
  "Final Approach...to Forever"
The Spy Who Loved Him #1052
**Twice in a Lifetime #1071
*Hot as Ice #1129
*Texas Hero #1165
*To Love a Thief #1225
§A Question of Intent #1255
§The Right Stuff #1279

Silhouette Books

Fortune's Children
Beauty and the Bodyguard

The Heart's Command
"Undercover Operations"

†Holiday Honeymoons:
  Two Tickets to Paradise
  "His First Father's Day"

In Love and War
"A Military Affair"

Silhouette Desire

Dreams and Schemes #872
†Halloween Honeymoon #1030
†Wrong Bride, Right Groom #1037
§Undercover Groom #1220
§Full Throttle #1556

Harlequin Historicals

††Alena #220
††Sweet Song of Love #230
††Siren's Call #236
His Lady's Ransom #275
Lady of the Upper Kingdom #320
Countess in Buckskin #396
The Tiger's Bride #423

Harlequin Books

Renegades
"The Rogue Knight"

Bride by Arrangement
"Mismatched Hearts"

The Gifts of Christmas
"A Drop of Frankincense"

The Officer's Bride
"The Major's Wife"

*Code Name: Danger
†Holiday Honeymoons
**Men of the Bar H
††Destiny's Women
§To Protect and Defend

MERLINE LOVELACE

spent twenty-three years in the air force, pulling tours in Vietnam, at the Pentagon and at bases all over the world. When she hung up her uniform, she decided to try her hand at writing. She's since had more than fifty novels published, with over seven million copies of her work in print. Watch for her next release, *Untamed,* coming from MIRA Books in September 2004.

To Maggie Price—friend, partner in crime and the world's greatest writer of romantic suspense. Thanks for all the quick reads and the great adventures!

Chapter 1

"Pegasus Control, this is Pegasus One."

"Go ahead, Pegasus One."

U.S. Coast Guard Lieutenant Caroline Dunn tore her gaze from the green, silent ocean flowing past the bubble cockpit of her craft. Her heart hammering against her ribs, she reported the statistics displayed on the brightly lit digital screens of the console.

"The Marine Imaging System reports a depth of eighty feet, with the ocean floor shelving upward at thirty degrees."

"That checks with our reading, Pegasus One. Switch to track mode at fifty feet."

"Aye, aye, Control."

Cari whipped her glance from the marine-data display to a screen showing a digital outline of her craft. There it was, the supersecret, all-weather, all-terrain, attack/assault vehicle code named *Pegasus*. It was in sea mode, a long, sleek tube with its wings swept back and tucked close to the hull. Those delta-shaped wings and their tilted rear engines would generate a crazy sonar signature, Cari thought with grim satisfaction. The enemy wouldn't know *what* the hell was coming at him.

Once *Pegasus* completed testing and was accepted for actual combat operations, that is. After months of successful—if often nerve-racking—land and air trials, *Pegasus* had taken his first swim at a fresh-water lake in New Mexico, close to its secret base.

Now the entire operation had moved to the south Texas coast and plunged the craft into deep water for the first time. It was Cari's job to take him down. And bring him back up!

Her palms tight on the wheel, she brought her glance back to the depth finder. "Seventy feet," she reported, her voice deliberately calm and measured.

"We copy that, Pegasus One."

Her steady tone betrayed none of the nervous excitement pinging around inside her like supercharged electrons. *Pegasus* had proved he could run like the wind and soar through the skies. In a few minutes, Cari would find out if the multi-purpose vehicle would perform as its designers claimed or sink like a stone to the ocean floor with her inside.

"Sixty," she announced.

"Confirming sixty feet."

The green ocean swirled by outside the pressurized canopy. A coast guard officer with more than a dozen years at sea under her belt, Cari had commanded a variety of surface craft. Her last command before joining the Pegasus test cadre was a heavily armed coastal patrol boat. This was the first time, though, she'd stood at the wheel of a vessel that operated equally well above *and* below the surface. *Pegasus* wouldn't dive as deep as a sub or skim across the waves as fast as a high-powered cutter, but it was the first military vehicle to effectively operate on land, in the air and at sea.

So far, anyway.

The big test was just moments away, when Cari cut the engines propelling *Pegasus* through the water and switched to track mode. In preliminary sea trials at New Mexico's Elephant Butte, the craft's wide-tracked wheels had dug into the lake bed, churned up mud and crawled right out of the water.

Of course, Elephant Butte was a relatively shallow lake. This was the ocean. The Gulf of Mexico, to be exact. With Corpus Christi Naval Air Station just a few nautical miles away, Cari reminded herself. The station's highly trained deep-water recovery team was standing by. Just in case.

Her gaze zeroed in on the depth finder. Silently she counted off the clicks. Fifty-five feet. Fifty-four. Three. Two...

"Pegasus One, shutting down external engines."

Dragging in a deep breath, Cari flicked the external power switch to Off. The engines mounted on the swept-back wings were almost soundless. Even at top speed they caused only a small, humming vibration. Yet with the absence of that tiny reverberation, the sudden, absolute silence now thundered in Cari's ears.

Momentum continued to propel *Pegasus* forward. Silent and stealthy as a shark after its prey, the craft cut through the green water. The depth finder clicked off another five meters. Ten. The sonar screen showed sloping ocean floor rising up to meet them dead ahead.

"Pegasus One switching to track mode."

With a small whir, the craft's belly opened. Its wide-track wheels descended. A few seconds later, the hard polymer rubber treads made contact with the ocean floor.

"Okay, baby," Cari murmured, half cajoling, half praying. "Do your thing."

A flick of another switch powered the internal engine. Biting down on her lower lip, Cari eased the throttle forward. *Pegasus* balked. Like a fractious stallion not yet broken to the bit, the craft seemed to dig in its heels. Then, after what seemed like two lifetimes, it responded to the firm hands on the reins.

The wheels grabbed hold. The vehicle began to climb. Fathom by fathom. Foot by foot. The water around Cari grew lighter, grayer, until she could see shafts of sunlight spearing through its surface.

A few moments later *Pegasus* gave a throaty growl of engines and broke through to the light. Waves slapped at the canopy and washed over the hull as Cari guided her craft toward a silver van positioned almost at water's edge. The mobile test control center had been flown in from New Mexico along with most of the personnel now manning it. They'd staked a claim to this isolated stretch of south Texas beach to conduct their deep-water sea trials. Heavily armed marines from the nearby naval air station patrolled the perimeter of the test site. The coast guard had added its small Padre Island fleet to the navy ships that kept fishing trawlers and pleasure craft away from the test sector.

By the time *Pegasus* roared out of the rolling surf, a small crowd of uniformed officers had spilled out of the van. They hurried across the hard-packed sand as Cari killed the engines. Blowing out a long breath, she patted the console with a hand that shook more than she wanted to admit.

"Way to go, *Pegasus*."

Her craft settled on the sand with a little hum, as if every bit as satisfied with its performance as she was. Smiling, Cari climbed out of the cockpit and made her way to the rear hatch. When she stepped into the bright sunlight, a tall blond god in an air force flight suit broke ranks with the rest of the uniformed officers. Ignoring the surf swirling around his black boots, he strode forward, wrapped his hands around Cari's waist and swung her to the sand.

"You took *Pegasus* for a helluva swim, Dunn!"

She grinned up at the sun-bronzed pilot. "Thanks, Dave. I think so, too."

The rest of the officers crowded around her. Army Major Jill Bradshaw shed her habitual reserve long enough to thump Cari on the back.

"Good job, roomie."

Lieutenant Commander Kate Hargrave, a senior weather scientist with the National Oceanographic and Atmospheric Service, hooked an arm around Cari's shoulders and gave her a fierce hug.

"I just about choked when the weather-service satellites picked up that squall developing out over the Gulf," the leggy redhead admitted. "What a relief it blew south, not north."

"No kidding!"

Doc Cody Richardson, the U.S. Public Health Service representative to the task force, ran an assessing glance over her face. In addition to providing expertise on the chemical, biological and nuclear defenses aboard the craft, the doc also acted as the cadre's chief medical officer.

"Did you experience any dizziness or nausea?"

"None," Cari replied, wiping out the memory of those few seconds of belly-clenching fear before *Pegasus* began his climb up the ocean floor.

Doc nodded, but she knew he'd be poring over the data with the bioengineers later to study her body's most minute reactions during various stages of the mission.

"Nice going, Dunn."

The gruff words swung her around. Major Russ McIver stood behind her, a solid six-two of buzz-cut marine. She and the major had locked horns more than once in the past few months. Mac's by-the-book, black-or-white view of the world allowed for no compromises and tended to ruffle even Cari's calm, usually un-rufflable temper.

This time, though, Mac was smiling at her in a way that made her breath catch. For a crazy moment, it might have been just the two of them standing on the beach with the surf lapping at their heels and the south Texas sky a bright, aching blue overhead.

Mac broke the spell. "Think you can get *Pegasus* to swim like that with a full squad of marines aboard?"

The crazy moment gone, Cari tugged off her ball

cap and raked back a few loose strands of her mink-brown hair. "No problem, Major. We'll add some ballast and take him out again tomorrow. Not much difference between a squad of marines and a boatload of rocks."

Mac started to respond to the good-natured gibe. The appearance of the navy officer in overall charge of the Pegasus project had him swallowing his retort.

Cari whipped up a smart salute, which Captain Westfall returned. His weathered cheeks creased into a broad grin. "Good run, Lieutenant."

"Thank you, sir."

"I could feel the salt water coursing through my veins the whole time you had *Pegasus* out there, testing his sea legs."

With the closest thing to a smirk the others had yet seen on the naval officer's face, Westfall reached out and patted the vehicle's steel hide. Cari hid a smile at his air of ownership and glanced around the circle of officers.

They represented all seven branches of uniformed services. Army. Navy. Air force. Marines. Coast guard. Public Heath Service. The National Oceanic and Atmospheric Administration.

Months ago they'd assembled in southeastern New Mexico. Since then they'd worked night and day alongside a similarly dedicated group of top-level ci-vilians to see *Pegasus* through its operational test phase. Now, with the deep-water tests underway, the end of their assignment loomed on the not-too-distant horizon.

Regret knifed through Cari at the thought. She'd grown so close to these people. She admired their dedication, cherished their friendship. The knowledge that their tight-knit group would soon break up was hard to take, even for an officer used to frequent rotations and new assignments.

Without thinking, she shifted her glance back to Russ McIver. Her stomach muscles gave a funny quiver as she took in the strong line of his jaw. The square, straight way he held himself. The bulge of muscles under the rolled-up sleeves of his camouflage fatigues, known for unfathomable reason as Battle Dress Uniform or BDUs.

Her regret dug deeper, twisted harder.

Frowning, Cari tried to shrug off the strange sensation. She had to get a grip here. This was just an assignment, one of many she'd held and would hold during her years in the U.S. Coast Guard. And Mac…

Mac was a colleague, she told herself firmly. A comrade in arms. Sometimes bullheaded. Often obnoxious, as those who see no shades of gray can be. But totally dedicated to the mission and the corps.

"It'll take an hour to download the data and run the post-test analyses." Captain Westfall checked his watch. "We'll conduct the debrief at thirteen-thirty."

"Aye, aye, sir."

An hour would give Cari plenty of time to draft her own post-test report. Still exhilarated by the success of her run, she headed for the silver van and its climate-controlled comfort. Early October in south Texas had proved far steamier than the high, dry desert of New Mexico.

Racks of test equipment, communications consoles and wide screens filled the front half of the van. The rear half served as a work and mini-conference area. Captain Westfall went forward to talk to the test engineers while the others filed into the back room. Eager to record her evaluation of the run, Cari settled at her workstation and flipped up the lid of her laptop. A blinking icon in the upper right corner drew her gaze.

She had e-mail.

None of the officers working on *Pegasus* could reveal their location or their activities. The techno-wizards assigned to the Pegasus project routed all communications with families, friends and colleagues through a series of secure channels that completely obscured their origin. For months, Cari's only link with the outside had been by phone or by e-mail.

She didn't have time to communicate with her large, widely dispersed circle of friends and family now, but she'd do a quick read to make sure no one was hurt or in trouble. A click of her mouse brought up a one-line e-mail.

Marry me, beautiful.

"Oh, hell."

She didn't realize she'd muttered the words out loud until Kate Hargrave glanced up from the work-station next to hers.

"Are you having trouble bringing up the post-run analysis screen? That last program mod is a bitch, in my humble opinion."

When Cari hesitated, reluctant to discuss personal matters in such a cramped setting, the weather officer scooted her chair over.

"Oh." Understanding flooded Kate's green eyes. "I see the problem. How are you going to answer him?"

Cari frowned at the screen. How the heck *was* she going to answer Jerry? She'd been dating the hand-some navy JAG off and on for almost a year. He was fun, sexy, and up for an appointment as a military judge. He was also the divorced father of three chil-dren. He'd learned the hard way how tough it was to sustain a two-career marriage. A bitter divorce had convinced him two careers, marriage *and* kids made the situation impossible.

Cari didn't want to admit he was right, but the fig-ures spoke for themselves. The divorce rate among the seagoing branches of the military was astronomical, almost twice the national norm. Long sea tours and frequent short notice deployments put severe strains on a marriage. If she wanted kids, which she most certainly did, something would have to give. Jerry and her parents—not to mention her own nagging conscience—suggested it should probably be her career in the coast guard.

Sighing, Cari fingered the mouse. "I don't know what I'm going to tell him," she murmured to Kate. "I have to think about it."

"What's to think?" Russ McIver put in sardonically from her other side. With a silent groan, Cari saw that he, too, had scooted his chair over, no doubt to check out the glitch with the troublesome new modification.

"The choice looks pretty clear to me," he drawled. "It's either yes or no."

Irritated that her private communication had become a matter of public discussion, she returned fire. "Why am I not surprised to hear that coming from you?"

Mac's hazel eyes hardened. Although Cari hadn't discussed her relationship with Jerry with anyone other than her roommates, there were few secrets in a group as small and tight as this one had become. Mac in particular had expressed little sympathy for Cari's personal dilemma. She might have guessed he wouldn't do so now.

"It's your decision," he said with a shrug. "Never mind that the coast guard selected you for promotion well ahead of your peers. It doesn't matter that you were chosen for a prestigious exchange tour with the British Coastal Defense Force. Or that you've racked up years in command of a ship and a crew. If pregnant, barefoot and permanent kitchen duty is what you want, Lieutenant, you should go for it."

Cari's brown eyes lasered into the marine's. "Last I heard, Major, it wasn't a court-martial offense to want to get married and have children. Nor is every woman who chooses to leave the service a traitor to her country."

The two other women officers present instantly closed ranks behind her.

"Lots of *men* leave the service," Jill Bradshaw pointed out acidly. A career army cop, she took few prisoners. "In fact, the first-term reenlistment rate for women is higher than it is for men."

"And in case you've forgotten," Kate Hargrave snapped, "the military is like any other organization. It's a pyramidal structure that requires a large base of Indians, with increasingly fewer chiefs at the more senior ranks. The services don't *want* everyone to stay in uniform."

Doc Richardson arched a brow and exchanged glances with USAF Captain Dave Scott. They were too wise—and had each grown too involved with one of the women now confronting McIver—to jump into this fray. Russ, however, appeared undaunted by the female forces arrayed against him.

"You're right," he agreed, refusing to retreat. "The military doesn't want everyone to stay in uniform. Only those who are good at what they do. So damned good they're hand-picked to field test a highly classified new attack/assault vehicle that could prove critical to future battlefield operations."

Cari clamped her mouth shut. She had no comeback for that. Neither did Kate or Jill. Like the male officers assigned to the Pegasus project, they'd been chosen based on their experience, expertise and ability to get things done. They *were* among the best their services had to offer and darn well knew it.

Still, she wasn't about to let the marine who alternately irritated, annoyed and attracted her have the last word.

"If *any* of us want to stay in uniform," she said tartly, "we'd better get off the subject of my personal life and onto the task at hand."

Swirling her chair around, she clicked the mouse to save Jerry's e-mail. She'd answer him later, when she figured out what the heck her answer would be. Another click brought up the analysis program. Wiping her mind clear of everything but the task at hand, she began drafting her preliminary post-mission report.

She was still hard at work when Captain Westfall wove his way through the racks of equipment to join his crew some time later. His expression was unexpectedly somber for a man who'd watched his baby perform flawlessly.

"Let me have your attention, people." His steel-gray eyes swept the crowded area, dwelling on each of his officers. "I've just received a coded communiqué from the Joint Chiefs of Staff. The Pegasus test cadre is being disbanded effective immediately."

Shock rippled through the group, along with a chorus of muttered exclamations.

"What the hell?"

"You're kidding!"

"Why?"

Captain Westfall stilled the clamor with an upraised hand.

"Our cadre has been redesignated. We're now the Pegasus Joint Task Force. Our mission is to extract two United States citizens trapped in the interior of Caribe."

The announcement burst like a cluster bomb among the stunned officers. Cari's mouth dropped open, snapped shut again, as her mind scrambled to switch from test to operational mode.

A map of Caribe flashed into her head. It was a small island nation, about sixty nautical miles off the coast of Nicaragua. Its internal political situation had been steadily worsening for months. The island's president for life was battling ferociously to hold on to his sinecure. In response to his repressive tactics, rebels had stepped up their action and the fight had turned bloody.

The Joint Chiefs of Staff had alerted Captain Westfall weeks ago about the possibility of using *Pegasus* to extract U.S. personnel, if necessary. As a result, he'd compressed the test schedule until it was so tight it squeaked. Evidently the deep-water sea trial Cari had just completed would be the final test. From now on, it was for real.

But two hours! That was short notice, even for a military deployment. Westfall made it clear they were to use that time to draw up an op plan.

"The U.S. began evacuation of its personnel this morning," he advised. "All are accounted for and are in various stages of departure except two missionaries. A squad of marines has gone into the interior after the missionaries and will escort them to a designated extraction site."

"I've flown over Caribe," Dave Scott commented grimly. "The jungle canopy is two or three hundred feet thick in places. Too thick to permit an extraction by air."

"And rebel forces now hold the one road in and out of the area," Captain Westfall confirmed. "The only egress is by river."

"Pegasus!" Cari breathed. "Now that he's demonstrated his sea legs, he's the perfect vehicle to use for an operation like this."

"Correct. Captain Scott, you'll fly *Pegasus* on the over-water leg from Corpus Christi to Nicaragua. Their government is maintaining a strict neutral position with regard to the political situation on Caribe but has given us permission to land at an unimproved airstrip just across the straits from the island."

Dave gave a quick nod. "I'll start working the flight plan."

"Once in Nicaragua, Lieutenant Dunn will pilot *Pegasus* to Caribe and navigate up the Rio Verde to a designated rendezvous point. Major McIver, your mission is to make contact with the marines and bring out the two stranded missionaries."

"Yes, sir."

"You'll be operating under strict rules of engagement," Westfall warned. "To avoid entangling the U.S. in the internal political struggle, you're not to fire lethal weapons unless under fire yourself. Questions?"

Her blood humming at the anticipation of action, Caroline joined the chorus of "No, sir!"

The steel-eyed navy officer turned away, swung back. His glance skimmed from Mac to Cari and back again.

"Things could turn ugly down there. Real ugly.

Make sure your next-of-kin notification data is up-to-date. You might also zap off a quick e-mail to your families,'' he added after a slight hesitation.

He didn't need to explain. Since 9/11, Cari had participated in enough short-notice deployments to know this might be her last communication with her folks for a while. Or her last, period.

Cari followed the captain's orders and zapped off one quick e-mail. Pumping pure adrenaline, she swung back around to find Mac contemplating her with a tight, closed expression.

''You didn't bat an eye at the prospect of going into Caribe.''

''Neither did you,'' she pointed out.

He hooked a thumb toward the now blank screen. ''What about Jerry-boy?''

Her shrug made the question irrelevant. This was what she'd trained for. This was what wearing a uniform entailed.

''Jerry isn't your concern. We've got work to do.''

Chapter 2

Mac couldn't believe it. Here he was, stuffing spare ammo clips into the pockets on his webbed utility belt, less than twenty minutes away from departing on a mission to extract U.S. citizens from a potentially explosive situation.

Yet for the first time in his life Mac couldn't force his mind to focus solely and exclusively on the task ahead. Every time he thought he'd crowded everything else out, the damned e-mail Cari had received a while ago would pop back into his head.

Marry me, beautiful.

What kind of a jerk proposed to a woman via e-mail? Particularly a woman like Caroline Dunn.

Mac had worked alongside a lot of professionals in the corps, male and female. The small, compact brunette currently frowning over a set of coastal navigational charts left most of them in the dust.

Hell, who was he kidding? Cari left *all* of them in the dust. He'd never met any woman with her combination of beauty and brains, and he'd tangled with more than his share. Particularly in his wilder days before the United States Marine Corps started him down a different path thirteen…no, fourteen years ago.

Fourteen years! Shaking his head, Mac shoved another spare clip into his belt. Hard to remember now how close he'd come to ending up on the wrong side of anyone in uniform. Harder still to remember the woman who'd almost put him there. He'd had no idea the thrill-seeking blonde who'd climbed on the back of his beat-up Harley was married to a California state senator. And he sure as hell hadn't known the woman was carrying a stash of Colombian prime in her fanny pack.

When the cops hauled the still underage Mac into her husband's office, the wealthy politician had given him a choice. A trumped-up possession charge and jail time or the United States Marines. It wasn't much of a choice. Mac had been staying just one step ahead of the law since flatly refusing to let the state put him in yet another foster home. He figured the marines would kick him out fast enough, just as his series of foster parents had.

Instead, the corps had molded a smart-mouthed punk into a single-minded, razor-edged fighting machine. In the often painful process, Mac found the home he'd never had. He'd also finished high school, earned a college degree, learned to lead as well as follow, and been chosen for Officers' Candidate School.

He'd never forget that crystal bright April morning at Quantico, when he'd raised his gloved hand to be sworn in as a commissioned officer. He took his oath to protect and defend the United States against all enemies *very* seriously. So, apparently, did Lieutenant Dunn. She'd served for more than ten years, had several command tours under her belt, and had played a key role in the war against terrorism during the coast guard's transition from the Treasury Department to the new Department of Homeland Security.

Yet here she was, actually debating whether to give up her career and her uniform to marry a smooth-talking JAG who'd probably never seen the business end of an assault rifle. The idea torqued Mac's jaws so tight he wasn't sure he'd ever get them unscrewed. They stayed locked the whole time Kate Hargrave and Cari pored over the charts.

''I've updated *Pegasus*'s onboard computers with Caribe's tidal patterns, riverine data and predicted climatic and atmospheric conditions,'' the weather officer was saying. ''You might see some swells from that squall on the way in, but rough weather shouldn't hit until you're on your way out.''

''How rough?''

''Better pack some extra barf bags for you and your passengers.''

''Oh, great!''

Shaking her head, Cari bent to stuff the charts in her gear bag. Her green-and-black jungle BDUs stretched taut over a trim, rounded rear. The enticing view had Mac grinding his teeth. Wrenching his glance away, he jammed another clip into his belt.

Okay. All right. He could admit it. The idea of Lieutenant Caroline Dunn marrying *anyone,* including a pansy-assed JAG, rubbed him exactly the wrong way. The woman had tied him up in knots more than once in the past few months. If he hadn't learned the hard way to avoid poaching on another man's territory—or if Cari had given the least hint she was interested in being poached on—he might have made a move on her himself.

But he had, and she hadn't.

With a little grunt, Mac reached for his assault rifle. He was checking the working parts when a low whine brought his head around.

Pegasus was spreading his wings. Like the mythical beast he'd been named for, the craft fanned out its delta-shaped fins. When they locked in place, the engines slowly tilted upright. Another whine, and the propellers unfolded like petals. In this configuration, *Pegasus* would lift straight up like a chopper. Once airborne, Dave would tilt the engines to horizontal and fly it like a fixed-wing aircraft.

The air force pilot was in the cockpit, clearly visible through the bubble canopy. Hooking a glance over his shoulder, he gave Captain Westfall a thumbs-up. The captain nodded and turned to Mac.

"Ready, Major?"

"Yes, sir."

"Lieutenant?"

"All set, sir."

Cari's calm reply did nothing to loosen the knots in Mac's chest. He'd been air-dropped into Afghanistan by a female USAF C-17 pilot. Had a bullet hole patched up by a particularly sexy navy nurse. Had relied on enlisted female marines to provide ground support and combat communications. He valued and respected the vital role women played in the military.

But this was the first time he was going into harm's way with a woman at his side. If she'd been anyone other than Caroline Dunn, the prospect might not have put such a kink in his gut.

Shouldering his assault rifle, he followed her through the open hatch.

* * *

Four hours later *Pegasus* was once again in sea mode—wings swept back, engines tilted rearward, propellers churning water like a ship's screws. Nicaragua lay well behind. Caribe was a gray smudge on the horizon. In between was a big stretch of open sea.

An increasingly turbulent sea, Cari noted.

"Kate was right on target," she commented, pitching her voice to be heard above the engines as she steered her craft through rolling green troughs. "Looks like we're starting to pick up some of the swells from that squall."

Mac responded with a grunt that earned him a quick glance. He didn't appear to appreciate the craft's agility to cut through the deepening troughs. In fact, he was looking distinctly green around the gills.

"The seas will probably get higher and rougher when we hit the barrier reef around the island," Cari advised. "You'd better pop a couple of those Dramamine pills Doc put in the medical kit."

"I'll make it."

"That wasn't a suggestion, Major."

The deceptively mild comment slewed Mac's head around. Cari could feel his gray-green eyes slice into her, but didn't bother to return the stare. He might outrank her on land. Aboard this craft, she was in command.

She kept her gaze on the gray smudge ahead as

Mac dragged out the medical kit. Only after he'd downed the pills as ordered did she slant him another glance. Like her, he was dressed for the jungle—web-sided boots, black T-shirt, black-and-green camouflage pants and shirt. Instead of a ball cap, though, a floppy-brimmed ''boonie'' hat covered his buzz-cut brown hair.

He looked leather tough and coldy lethal. *Not* someone you wanted to suddenly come nose to nose with in the jungle. Cari had to admit she was glad they were on the same side for this operation.

''Is this freshening sea going to slow us down?'' he asked with an eye to the digital map displayed on the instrument panel.

Their course was highlighted in glowing red. It took them straight across the fifty-mile stretch of open water, through the outer reef encircling Caribe and into a small bay on the southern tip of the palm-shaped island. Once inside the bay, they'd aim for the mouth of the Rio Verde and head some twenty-six miles upriver.

''*Pegasus* can handle these swells,'' Cari said in answer to his question. ''We should arrive right on target.''

''Good enough. I'll confirm with Second Recon.''

He'd already established contact with the six-man reconnaissance team that had been sent into the jungle to retrieve the American missionaries. Luckily, they were equipped with CSEL—the new Combat Survivor/Evader Locator. Not much larger than an ordinary cell phone, the handheld radio provided over-the-horizon data communications, light-of-sight voice modes, and precise GPS positioning and land navigation. The handy-dandy new device was state-of-the-art and just off the assembly line. Neither the rebel nor government forces in Caribe could intercept or interpret its secure, scrambled transmissions.

"Second Recon, this is Pegasus One."

"This is Second Recon. Go ahead, Pegasus."

The marine in charge of the reconnaissance team sounded so young, Cari thought. And so grimly determined.

"Be advised we're twenty nautical miles off the coast of Caribe and closing fast," Mạc informed him. "We're holding to our ETA."

"We copy, Pegasus. We're about five klicks from the target."

Five kilometers from the mission put them about eight from the river, Cari saw in another quick glance at the digital display. The marines still had some jungle to hack through.

"We'll bundle up our charges as soon as we reach the target and proceed immediately to the designated rendezvous point," the team leader promised.

"Roger, Second. We'll be waiting for you."

Frowning, Mac took a GPS reading on the team's

signal and entered its position with a few clicks of the keyboard built into the instrument console. His frown deepened as *Pegasus* plowed into another trough. The hull hit with a smack that sent spray washing over the canopy.

"The swells are getting heavier."

"They are," Cari agreed.

He shot her a hard look. "Can't we put on a little more speed? I don't want to leave those marines sitting around, twiddling their thumbs with the rebel forces combing the jungle for them."

"We won't."

The calm reply brought his brows snapping together under the brim of his hat. "Are you that sure of yourself or is this the face you put on when you're in command?"

"Yes, I'm sure," she answered, "and what you see is what you get."

For the first time since they'd departed Corpus Christi, Mac relaxed into a grin. "From where I'm sitting," he drawled, "what I see looks pretty good."

Her hands almost slid off the throttle. "Good grief! Is that a compliment?"

"It is."

A tiny dart of pleasure made it past the butterflies beating against Cari's ribs. After all these weeks of butting heads with the stubborn marine, she hadn't expected any warm fuzzies just moments away from entering a potential hostile fire zone. Her brief pleasure took a back seat to business when she checked the displays and saw they'd entered Caribe's territorial waters.

"We're within twelve miles of the island. We'll hit the coral reef in a few minutes. You'd better get ready for a bumpy ride."

Bumpy didn't begin to describe it.

Waves pounded the sunken coral reef. The swells that had kept Mac's stomach churning became monster waves. The huge walls of green curled and crashed and roared like the hounds of hell. He clamped his jaw shut and tried not to wince at the vicious battering *Pegasus* took.

Cari, he noted, didn't so much as break a sweat as she worked the throttle and wheel. Somehow she managed to dodge the worst of the monsters while keeping her craft aimed straight for the calmer waters inside the reef.

Finally, *Pegasus* broke through the pounding surf. Mac mouthed a silent prayer of relief and swiped the sweat off his forehead with a forearm. Squinting through the canopy, he searched the vegetation fronting the beach for some sign of an opening.

"We're right on track according to the GPS coordinates," Cari confirmed after another read of the instruments. "The river mouth should lie dead ahead."

"Bring us in closer."

Keeping a wary eye on the depth finder, she took *Pegasus* into the bay. "The ocean floor's shelving fast. If we don't find the mouth soon, I'll have to switch to track mode and take us…"

"There it is."

The narrow gap in the tangled vegetation was almost invisible. Mac would have missed it if not for the rippling water surface where the river eddied into the bay.

Getting a lock on the ripples, Cari swung the wheel. Moments later, *Pegasus* was fighting his way against the powerful current. Before the green gloom of the river swallowed them, Mac needed to advise the recon team they were on their way up the Verde.

"Second Recon, this is Pegasus One."

He waited for a reply. None came. Frowning, he keyed his mike again.

"Second Recon, this is Pegasus One. Acknowledge please."

Long, tense seconds of silence passed. Cari pulled her gaze from the instruments. Mac saw his own mounting worry mirrored in her brown eyes. His jaw tightening, he was about to try again when the unmistakable rattle of gunfire came bursting through the radio. The patrol leader came on a second later, his voice sharp-edged but remarkably calm given the stutter of small arms fire in the background.

"Pegasus One, this is Second Recon. Be advised we've run smack into a heavily armed rebel patrol."

"Do you have them in your sights?"

"We do, but our orders are to avoid returning fire unless under extreme duress."

The sergeant broke off, cursing as another loud burst made extreme duress sound a whole lot closer than it had a few seconds ago. Mac's fists went white at the knuckles. Those were marines taking fire. He didn't breathe until the team leader came back on the horn.

"We can give these bastards the slip, but we'll have to fall back. We'll try to lead them as far as possible away from the target. Sorry, One. Looks like you're on your own from here on out."

"Roger that."

"Good luck, sir."

"You, too."

The transmission cut off. The sudden silence drowned out even the muted whine of *Pegasus*'s engines. His jaw locked tight, Mac took another GPS reading from the radio signal and noted the team's position on his map. They were still a good four klicks away from the mission.

"We've entered the river channel. I'm going to take us under, then power up to full speed."

The calm announcement brought Mac's head snapping around. Cari's profile was outlined against the dark vegetation lining the riverbank. She kept her attention divided between the instrument panel and the view outside the bubble canopy, now narrowed to a fast-flowing river crowded above and on both sides by jungle.

She had every intention of pushing ahead, with or without fire support from the squad of marines they'd planned to rendezvous with. Evidently, it hadn't occurred to her to abandon their mission. It hadn't occurred to Mac, either, until this moment.

"Listen up, Lieutenant. We need to take another look at our operations plan. I…"

"Don't even think it."

The flat comeback snapped his brows together, but she didn't give him time to respond. Slewing around, she raked him with a wire-brush look.

"This is a two-person operation, McIver. If you go in, I go in."

He bit back the reminder that he was in command of the land phase of this mission. He knew damn well she'd remind *him* he hadn't yet set foot on dry land.

Satisfied she'd made her point, Cari prepared to take *Pegasus* under the river's green surface.

Twenty-six torturous miles later, she brought her craft up from the murky depths. Cari had seen more than her fill of submerged tree stump, twisting roots, slime-covered boulders and darting water snakes.

Once above the surface, the jungle reached out to envelop them. When the water sluiced off the canopy, Cari got the eerie feeling she and Mac were alone in a dark, still universe. Only an occasional stray sunbeam penetrated the dense overgrowth hundreds of feet above. Strangler vines drooped down like ropes from entwined branches. Giant ferns fanned out to cover the riverbanks.

Carefully, Cari navigated the last few yards to their designated rendezvous point. No one was waiting on the riverbank. No marines. No missionaries. No rebels or government troops.

Mac swept both banks with high-powered Night Vision goggles. The goggles could penetrate the gloom beyond the banks far better than the human eye.

"It looks clear," he said tersely.

Cari nodded. "Hold tight."

Repeating the process she'd tested only this morning in the Gulf waters just off Corpus Christi, she switched *Pegasus* from sea to land mode. The outer engines shut down and tucked against the hull. The propellers folded. The belly doors opened and the wide-track wheels descended.

Like some primeval beast crawling up out of the swamp, *Pegasus* clawed his way up the riverbank. The wheel tread ate up the giant ferns and spit them out. But even a high-tech, all-terrain, all-weather assault vehicle was no match for the impenetrable jungle.

Mac would have to hoof it from here. Killing the engines, Cari hit the switch to open the rear hatch. Smothering tropical heat instantly rushed in. So did an astonishing variety of flying insects. Swatting at a winged critter in a particularly virulent shade of orange, Cari climbed out of her seat and followed Mac to the hatch.

"I'll bring out the two Americans," he told her. "You stay with *Pegasus*."

She swallowed her instinctive protest. With her craft secured and on dry land, the baton had passed. She was no longer in command. From now until Mac returned with the missionaries, this was his show.

Feeling a little deflated, she watched as he hunkered down on his heels and dug through his pack. A few, quick smears decorated his face in shades of green and black. Thin black gloves covered his hands. He performed a radio check, chambered a round in his assault rifle, and slung the weapon over his shoulder. His gray-green eyes lasered into her as he confirmed their communications pattern.

"I'll signal you at half-hour intervals. If I miss one signal, wait another half hour. If I miss two, get the hell out of Dodge. Understand?"

"Yes."

His gaze speared into her. "I mean it, Dunn. No stupid heroics. They could get us both killed."

He was right. She knew he was right. Yet her throat closed at the thought of leaving him in this smothering heat and darkness.

"Two missed signals and you're gone. Got that, Lieutenant?"

She gave a tight nod. He returned it with a jerk of his chin and started off. He took two steps, only two, and swung back.

"What the hell."

The muttered oath had Cari blinking in surprise. She blinked again when he strode back to her and caught her chin in his hand.

"Mac, what are—?"

His mouth came down on hers, hard and hot and hungry. Stunned, she stood stiff as an engine blade while his lips moved over hers. A moment later, he faded into the jungle. She was left with the tang of camouflage face paint in her nostrils and the taste of Mac on her lips.

Chapter 3

"That was smart, McIver. Really smart."

Thoroughly disgusted with himself, Mac moved through the dense undergrowth. He'd made some questionable moves in his life. Tangling with the senator's wife had been one of them. Laying that kiss on Caroline Dunn was another. What was this thing he had for married—or almost married—women?

Calling himself an idiot one more time, Mac forced his thoughts away from the woman, the kiss and the heat that brief contact had sent spearing right through his belly.

The mission lay some three kilometers from the river. Five or six kilometers beyond that Second Recon had run smack into a heavily armed rebel force. The marines had said they'd fall back and draw the rebels away from the mission, but Mac wasn't taking any chances. He kept his tread light on the damp, spongy earth and his assault weapon at the ready as he pushed through the giant ferns.

Once away from the river, the ferns thinned and the going got easier. The overhead canopy was so thick only the occasional stray sunbeam could penetrate. It was like moving through a dim, cavernous cathedral with tall columns of trees spearing straight up to support the vaulted ceiling. The deep shadows provided excellent concealment for him and, unfortunately, for potential enemies.

He pushed on, using the GPS built into his handheld digital radio to check his position and send Cari a silent signal at the prearranged times. With each step, his jumpy nerves steadied and his concentration narrowed until there was only Mac, his weapon and the gloom ahead.

As swift and stealthy as a panther, he cut through the jungle. Every sense had moved to full alert, every flutter of an orange-winged butterfly and slither of a spotted lizard sent a message. So did the sudden, raucous screech of a parrot.

Mac spun to his right, dropped into a crouch, and caught a flash of scarlet as the bird took wing. Peering into the gloom, Mac tried to see what had spooked it. Nothing else moved. No leafy ferns swayed.

Forcing the knotted muscles at the base of his skull to relax, Mac came out of the crouch. Without warning, something hard and sharp smacked into his forehead just above his right eyebrow.

Cursing, he ignored the blood pouring into his eye and aimed his assault rifle at the base of a hollow-trunked strangler fig. When the shadows moved, his finger went tight on the trigger.

"Whoever's in there better show yourself. Now!"

He repeated the warning in Spanish and was searching for the few words of Caribe he'd memorized when another missile came zinging at him. This one he managed to dodge. It ricocheted off the tree behind him and landed at his feet.

A rock! Mac saw in disgust. Damned if he'd hadn't taken a direct hit from a rock.

"You've got five seconds to show yourself," he shouted, blinking away the blood. "Four, three, two…"

The shadow burst out of the tree trunk. With a frightened look at the gun aimed at his chest, the attacker whirled and ran.

With another muttered curse, Mac eased the pressure on the trigger. His assailant was a kid. A scrawny, barefooted kid in a Spider-Man T-shirt, of all things. Judging by his size, the runt couldn't be more than six or seven.

"Hey! Hold on! I won't hurt you!"

Fumbling for the Spanish phrases, he hotfooted it after the kid. He couldn't have him spreading the word that there was an armed *Americano* roaming loose in the neighborhood. Not until after Mac had departed the scene with the two missionaries, anyway.

His longer legs ate up the ground. He caught the kid by the back of his ragged shirt and swung him around. The little stinker put up a heck of a fight, grunting and kicking and jabbing with his bony elbows. Keeping well clear of those sharp elbows, Mac held him at arm's length.

"I'm a friend. Amigo."

The kid twisted frantically. He wasn't buying the friend bit. Considering the violence now ripping his country apart, Mac couldn't exactly blame him. He gave the boy a quick little shake.

"Where's your village? *¿Dónde está su,* uh, *casa?*"

Still the youngster wouldn't answer. His lower lip jutted out and his black eyes shot daggers at the marine, but he refused to speak so much as a word. Instead, he made some motion with his hand that Mac strongly suspected was the Caribe version of buzz off, pal.

"Stubborn little devil, aren't you?"

Well, no matter. He had to be from the village where the Americans had set up their mission. It was the only settlement in this vicinity.

Bunching his fist, Mac kept a firm grip on the boy's shirt with one hand while he slung his weapon over his shoulder and probed the cut above his eye with the other. The skin was tender and already rising to a good-sized lump, but the blood had slowed to a trickle. He'd clean the cut when he got to the village. Unless the navigational finder in his radio was sending faulty signals, it couldn't be much farther.

It wasn't.

Another ten minutes brought Mac and his sullen, squirming captive to the edge of a clearing. Although the boy hadn't as yet uttered a single sound, Mac clamped a hand over his mouth. Eyes narrowed, he surveyed the scene.

It didn't take him long to determine the village was deserted. No dogs yapped. No pigs snuffled in the dirt. No goats were tethered to stakes beside the huts. Nor could Mac discern any sign of human habitation…until an unmistakably female figure in a sleeveless white blouse and baggy tan slacks emerged from the clapboard building at the far end of the dirt track that served as the village's main thoroughfare. Obviously agitated, the woman thrust a hand through her cropped blond hair.

"Paulo! Where are you?"

The woman repeated the shout in Spanish, then Caribe. Mac was congratulating himself on having located at least one of the missionaries when his attacker gave a strangled grunt and renewed his frenzied attempts to escape.

This time, Mac let him go. The little squirt shot off, his skinny legs pumping.

"Paulo! There you are!"

Her shoulders sagging in relief, the woman dropped to her knees and opened her arms. The boy charged straight into them. The woman hugged him fiercely, rocking back and forth.

Mac decided he'd better make his presence known before the kid painted him as an enemy. But when he stepped out from behind the tree, the woman's horrified glance whipped from his black-painted, blood-streaked face to his assault rifle. Before Mac could identify himself and assure her he meant no harm, she let loose with a piercing yell.

"¡Los soldados!"

"Lady, it's okay. I'm…"

He started toward her, then stopped dead as the shutters covering the windows of one of the huts banged open. In the ominous silence that followed, he heard the snick of a weapon being cocked.

Impatiently, Cari swatted at a persistent mosquito and searched the towering ferns lining the river.

Where the heck was Mac?

Why hadn't he contacted her in… She drew another bead on the functional black watch strapped to her wrist. In fifty-two minutes?

After he'd missed his last signal, she'd waited ten endless minutes before trying to raise him on his radio. When another ten had crawled by, she'd tried again. Each time she'd received nothing. Nada. Zilch.

Now she was eight minutes away from the point where he'd insisted she get out of Dodge.

Could she abandon him?

She was no closer to an answer now than she'd been for the past fifty-three minutes. She glowered at the leafy ferns, willing them to part.

Dammit, where was he?

And what the heck had that kiss been all about?

She didn't have an answer for either question.

Grinding her back teeth in frustration, Cari pulled out her sidearm and released the magazine. A quick check verified the clip was full. She snapped it back in, holstered the Beretta, and swiped her damp, sweaty palms down the side of her BDU shirt.

She could still taste him on her lips. Still feel the scrape of his bristly chin on hers. With all her years in uniform, she would never have imagined she'd be feeling this kind of prickly, itchy, physical awareness smack in the middle of a mission!

Or at all, for that matter.

She was no nun. She'd dated her share of smart, sexy men. Had drifted in and out of several heavy relationships before meeting Jerry. And he was certainly no slouch when it came to stirring her senses. Yet Cari was darned if she could remember ever experiencing such a severe reaction to a single kiss.

She'd be a fool to attach too much significance to it, though. It could only have sprung from tension, that peculiar combination of nerves and adrenaline that came at times like this. Mac had no interest in her outside the professional. None he'd demonstrated during their months in the New Mexico desert, anyway. And she found him almost as irritating as she did attractive.

So why the heck couldn't she lick his taste from her lips? Scowling, she slapped a palm against the side of the hatch.

Where *was* he!

"Pegasus One, this is Two."

The sharp, clear communication almost had Cari jumping out of her skin. Gulping down her relief, she keyed her radio.

"Go ahead, Two."

"Be advised that I'm en route back to your position, approximately fifty meters out. Prepare to cast off as soon as we get our passengers on board."

"Roger."

He'd done it! He'd located the missionaries and

brought them out. Cari would have a word with him later about the grief his missed signal had put her through. Right now, she had to power up her craft.

The engines were humming and she was back at the open hatch when the ferns began to shake. Seconds later, Mac popped through the leafy wall. He was carrying something on his back. Not something, Cari saw in surprise when he turned to hold aside the ferns. Someone. A child.

A woman pushed through the greenery after Mac. She was followed by a boy in sneakers and scruffy, white cotton pants. Another child poked through a second later, this one a scrawny girl in pigtails and tattered, pink sneakers.

Her jaw dropping, Cari watched as several more children emerged. A tall, lanky man with a wide-eyed little girl on his shoulders brought up the rear of the column. Mac hustled them all toward the waiting craft.

The woman reached the vehicle first. Cari stretched down a hand, grasped her wrist, and helped her up the steps.

"Thanks." She raked a hand through short, sweat-spiked blond bangs. "I'm Dr. White. Janice White."

"Glad you made it, Doc."

Nodding, the missionary stood back as Cari reached for the child Mac lifted up. He was a tousled-haired boy of three or four. He was also blind, Cari realized when his groping hands failed to connect with hers. Gulping, she took a better stance and stretched out her arms. His chubby fingers found her sleeves and dug in.

"Okay, I've got him."

To her consternation, she soon discovered each of the children possessed some form of physical disability. One dragged his right leg. Another had a cleft palate that left his young face tragically disfigured. The merry gap-toothed girl had a spine so twisted she couldn't stand upright. Dismayed, Cari waited for Mac to climb aboard.

"I had to bring them," he said in response to her silent query. "The Whites wouldn't leave them."

Dragging off his boonie hat, he swiped an arm across his sweat-drenched face. Only then did Cari see the vicious-looking cut on his forehead. Someone—Dr. White, she guessed—had added a few neat stitches. Before Cari could ask Mac what he'd run into, the tall, lanky missionary grabbed her hand and pumped it.

"I'm Reverend Harry White. I can't tell you how grateful we are to you for coming after us. The fighting in the area drove off the villagers weeks ago. We had no one to help us bring the children through the jungle."

"Yes, well…"

"Our church has arranged adoptions for them, you

see. My sister and I have been trying to get them to the States for almost two years.''

"Sister?''

Cari's glance cut to the doctor. She'd assumed—they'd all assumed—the Whites were husband and wife. Obviously the intelligence supplied for this hastily mounted operation had missed a few minor details.

''We've paid a fortune in bribes,'' Janice White put in, picking up on her brother's comment. ''Obviously not to the right people.''

''No matter,'' the reverend said with a smile. ''We're on our way now.''

''Hang on a minute!''

Cari shot a quick glance at Mac. His shrug indicated he'd already covered this ground once with the Whites. Biting her lip, she faced the minister.

''Are you suggesting we smuggle these kids out of Caribe?''

''Yes,'' the man of God replied simply.

Cari pursed her lips. She was an officer in the United States Coast Guard. A major portion of her job was to prevent the kind of illegal emigration the missionary was suggesting. She'd lost count of the number of vessels crammed with refugees she and other coast guard crews had been forced to turn back. Small boats carrying whole families across miles of open sea. Fishing trawlers trying to slip fifty or so desperate souls past coastal patrols. Container ships with hidden compartments stuffed with starving, suffocating cargo.

"Smuggling them out is our only recourse at this point," Reverend White said earnestly. "As Janice said, we've been working on their papers for more than two years. Finding a responsible official to deal with was difficult enough before the fighting erupted. Now, it's well nigh…"

"Harry!"

His sister's frantic cry jerked the missionary around.

"Where's Paulo?"

"Isn't he with you?"

"No."

"Dear Lord above!" The reverend spun back to Mac, his face contorted with panic. "He was right ahead of me. I can't imagine how… When…"

"I'll find him," Mac said grimly. His glance cut to Cari. "You'd better get *Pegasus* ready to swim. I picked up some radio chatter a while back. It sounded close. So close I didn't want to risk using my own radio until I knew I could get the kids safely aboard."

Well, that explained why he'd skipped an interim signal. Unfortunately, the explanation didn't particularly sit well with Cari. The idea that the bad guys were poking around nearby upped her pucker factor considerably. Climbing over kids and backpacks, she made her way to the cockpit.

Scant minutes later she had *Pegasus* ready to plunge back into the river. He sat nosed half on, half off the bank. Cari kept the engines churning gently in reverse, with just enough power to keep her craft from being dragged along with the current. The rear hatch remained open. All the while her heart pounded out the seconds until Mac returned.

She hated this business of being left behind. She was used to sailing her ship, her crew and herself into action, not sitting at the controls while someone else took the lead. She wanted in on the action.

Mac had been right, she thought grimly. She wasn't the barefoot, pregnant and in the kitchen type. As much as she ached for a child of her own, she knew she belonged right here, right now. No one else could have maneuvered *Pegasus* up this narrow, twisting river. No one else could get it back down.

Which she hoped to do.

Like, *soon!*

They only had a few hours of daylight left. She didn't relish navigating the Rio Verde in the dark, even with all the sophisticated instrumentation crammed into *Pegasus*. It was time to make tracks.

Where the heck was Mac?

He came crashing through the ferns several heart-pounding minutes later. He had a scruffy little boy tucked under one elbow and his assault rifle tight in the crook of the other. Cari's breath wheezed out on a small sigh of relief.

The next instant, she sucked it back in again. Right before her eyes, the fronds above Mac's head began to dance wildly. A heartbeat later, she heard the deadly splat, splat, splat of bullets tearing through the leaves.

He was taking fire!

Twisting in her seat, Cari shouted a terse order. "Dr. White! Reverend! Get the children down flat on the deck! Now!"

She waited only long enough to see Mac and the kid come diving through the rear opening. Slewing back around, she hit the switch to close the hatch, wrapped her fist around the throttles and thrust the engines to full forward.

Pegasus sailed off the bank. His belly hit the river's surface with a smack that would have rattled Cari's teeth if she hadn't already clenched them tight. Her jaw locked, she aimed her craft for the dark, rushing channel in the middle of the river.

She expected to hear bullets pinging off the canopy at any second. The bubble was made of some new composite that was supposed to be able to withstand a direct hit from a mortar, but she wasn't particularly anxious to test the shield's survivability.

She made it to midstream without any bullets cracking against the canopy. As soon as the depth finder registered enough clearance, she took *Pegasus* under.

The water closed around them. The view ahead became one of swirling currents, darting fish and dark, fuzzy shapes. As she had during the torturous journey upriver, Cari kept her gaze locked on the sonar screen. All she needed to do now was ram a jagged stump or slimy green bolder.

She didn't relax her vigil until Mac slid into the seat beside her and assumed duties as navigator. Blowing out a ragged breath, Cari slanted him glance.

"Is the kid okay?"

"Yeah. He's a tough little runt." A rueful smile flitted across Mac's face. "He's the one who put this crease in my forehead."

"How'd he do that?"

"He beaned me with a rock."

Despite the tension still stringing her as tight as an anchor cable, Cari had to laugh. "That's going to make a great story at the bar when we get back to base. So what happened? How did you lose him?"

"My guess is he fell back and couldn't call out to us to wait for him."

"Couldn't?"

Mac's smile faded. "When I first collared the kid, I tried to get him to tell me his name and where he'd sprung from. He got stubborn and clammed up. Or so I thought. It wasn't until Doc White was stitching me

up that I found out he can't talk. He was born without
a larynx.''

"Oh, no!''

"The most he can manage is an occasional grunt.''

Cari slumped back against her seat. Her stab of pity
for the little boy battled with practical reality.

"You know the crap is going to hit the fan big-
time if we take these kids out of Caribe without au-
thorization from their government.''

"Maybe.''

"There's no maybe about it. Remember the international furor over the Cuban kid, Elian Gonzales?''

"There's a difference here. Elian Gonzales had a
father who wanted him back. These kids are orphans.
Throwaways, as Janice White described them, probably because of their disabilities. If their government
had bothered with them at all, they would have been
shuffled into some institution or foster home.''

A muscle ticked in the side of his jaw. For a moment his expression was remote, closed, unreadable.
Then he tore his gaze away from the screen. The hard
edges to his face softened and he gave Cari a quick,
slashing grin.

"I say we take them out with us.''

She fell a little in love with him at that moment.
Here he was, the all-or-nothing, you're-in-or-you're
out, gung ho marine, putting his military career on
the line for a boatload of kids.

Only belatedly did she remember she'd be putting her career on the line, too.

Oh, well. If she'd learned nothing else during her years of service, she'd discovered it was a whole lot easier to ask for forgiveness after the fact than obtain permission beforehand.

"Seeing as they're already on board," she replied with an answering grin, "I say we take them with us, too. But I'll let you advise Captain Westfall of our additional passengers," she tacked on hastily.

Chapter 4

Cari was actually starting to believe she'd get her craft and its passengers safely away from Caribe when disaster struck. Unfortunately, she didn't realize that hazy blur dead ahead represented disaster until it was too late.

"What the heck...?"

That was all she got out before *Pegasus* plowed into what looked very much like a net. It *was* a net, she discovered as the prow pushed hard against the barrier. Made of thin, loosely woven vines. No wonder it hadn't returned any kind of a sonar signature.

The vines snared *Pegasus* like a giant fish, held him for a moment, then yielded to his powerful forward momentum. The net ripped apart. The vessel's prow poked through. A long length of the hull followed. The swept-back wings and rear-tilted engines, however, snagged on the tangled remnants of the netting.

"Hell!"

Cari yanked the throttle back and reversed thrust, but it was too late. Dangling vines had wrapped tight around the propeller shafts. The twin engines gave a little sputter and died.

For a moment there was only silence.

Dead silence.

Cari felt a bubble of panic rise in her throat. Sailors the world over had nightmares about just this kind of a situation. She was trapped underwater. With her boat experiencing total engine failure.

As quickly as it rose, her panic evaporated. She shot a glance at the depth finder and confirmed they were less than ten feet below the river's surface. Even without engines, she could float *Pegasus* up enough to pop the canopy and check out the situation.

"We'll have to surface," she told Mac.

"Not until we figure out what the heck snared us," he returned, craning his neck to peer through the gloom at the entangling vines.

"My guess is it's a fishing net."

"Why didn't we hit it coming upriver?"

"Could be the locals only string it in the afternoon, when the river's running with the tide."

"Or it could be a trap set specifically for us."

The same possibility had occurred to Cari. "I don't think so," she said, chewing on the inside of her lip. "We swam upriver underwater. As far as we know, no one observed us going in."

"Someone sure as hell observed us coming out. Those weren't bees buzzing around my head back there."

"They saw *you,* but I don't think they saw *Pegasus.* We got you aboard and went under before whoever was taking potshots at you charged through the ferns."

Mac's eyes narrowed. "All anyone needed was a glimpse. Just a glimpse. They could have radioed to their buddies downriver, had them string a net."

The terse exchange helped resolve some of the awful doubts gnawing at Cari. "Their buddies couldn't have chopped down vines and strung something this elaborate in an hour. My guess...my considered opinion," she amended, "is that we'll soon come face-to-face with some local fishermen who are going to be very surprised at what they've netted."

By now the questions were coming at her from the Whites as well. "What's happened?" the reverend called anxiously from the back.

"Why are we stopped?" his sister wanted to know.

"We hit a net," Cari called back. "A fisherman's

net I think, and fouled the engines. We'll have to surface and try to clear them.''

Slowly, foot by foot, Cari floated *Pegasus* up from the murky depths.

The canopy broke the surface first. Eyes narrowed, shoulders tense, Mac twisted around and did a swift three-sixty. The only signs of life he spotted were two red-furred monkeys hanging from a branch extending over the river. The creatures ceased their antics and gaped at the monster rising from the depths before emitting high-pitched shrieks of alarm and scrambling away.

Pegasus pawed his way up inch by inch. Still tethered by the net, the craft remained caught in midcurrent. The swift moving river flowed past, rushing over the wings, swirling just a few inches below the canopy.

Cari assessed the situation once again and saw only one option. ''I'm going to pop the canopy and try to cut through the vines.''

Mac shot her a swift look. ''You sure opening the canopy won't flood us?''

''Pretty sure.''

The possibility she might be putting the children at grave risk generated a sick feeling in the pit of her stomach. She saw no other way to free her craft, however. It was either pop the canopy and cut the vines or drift at the end of this tether indefinitely.

"Go back and tell the Whites what we're doing," she instructed Mac. "Stay with them and be prepared to pass the children up through the cockpit if we start to take on water. Worst-case scenario, we swim them to shore."

He nodded, not questioning her decision or authority, and climbed out of his seat. When he signaled that they were ready in the rear compartment, Cari hit the button to raise the canopy.

The hydraulic lift pushed the nose down a few inches. River water rushed in, soaking her from the waist down. After a heart-stopping second or two, the nose bobbed upward again and the flood ceased.

"All right," she breathed. "Okay."

She unhooked her seat harness, her fingers shaking a little. Nothing like almost sinking a ship and its passengers to take the starch out of a girl.

"I'll crawl out onto the wings and assess the damage," she told Mac when he climbed back in the cockpit. "You'd better get on the radio and advise base we've, ah, hit a slight snag."

Her feeble attempt at a pun fell flat. Mac didn't crack so much as a shadow of a smile. Shrugging, Cari unbuckled her harness and hooked a leg over the side of the cockpit. Once on the swept-back wing, she dropped to all fours.

The swirling river water turned the wing slick and the going tricky, but she made it to the half-submerged engine without too much difficulty. A single glance at the vines wrapped tight around the propeller shaft had her muttering a smothered curse.

The vines were as thick as her wrist. She'd need a chain saw to hack through them. Unfortunately, the emergency equipment aboard *Pegasus* didn't include a chain saw. A fire axe, yes. An acetylene torch. An assortment of other tools, hoses and spare electronic parts. But no chain saw.

Balancing carefully on all fours, Cari traced the path of the twisted vine cable that formed the spine of the net. It was anchored to trees on either side of the river. Maybe she could use the axe to chop through one end. The other end would then act as an anchor chain and swing *Pegasus* in a wide arc toward the opposite bank. Once in shallow water, she could try to unfoul the engines.

It might work. It had to work. She wasn't going to abandon a multimillion-dollar prototype vehicle to the river gods unless she had no other choice.

Before she tried to salvage her craft, though, she wanted the Whites and the children ashore.

Mac went first to reconnoiter.

Using the vine cable to pull himself through the water, he swam to the left bank and clambered up.

Once again, he disappeared into the thick greenery lining the river's edge. The seconds crawled by. Stretched into minutes. Cari was sweating profusely from the oppressive jungle heat and stomach-twisting tension when he reappeared.

Gulping, she saw he prodded three wide-eyed, dis-believing fishermen ahead of him at gunpoint. Mouths agape, they stared at the monster they'd snared in their net.

"Their village is about fifty yards in from the river," Mac shouted to Cari. "Get Reverend White up to the cockpit so we can communicate with these guys and determine whether they're friend or foe."

Harry White soon ascertained they were friends. Or at least they claimed no recent contact with either government forces or the rebels waging vicious gue-rilla warfare in the area. The reverend also extracted an offer of food and shelter for the night that would soon drop over the island like a blanket. Still wary but trusting to instincts that said the villagers repre-sented no immediate threat, Mac holstered his side-arm and organized the process of ferrying the children to shore.

Cari was the last to leave her craft. Plunging into the river, she used the net to pull herself hand over hand to dry land. Once there, she stayed to keep a watchful eye on the vehicle while Mac, Harry and Janice White shepherded the children to the village.

Mac returned with what had to be most, if not all, of the local population. Agog, they gaped at the long, sleek craft trapped in what remained of the net. Several villagers jumped into the river and paddled out for a closer look.

Using Harry White as an interpreter, Cari explained her idea of hacking through the far side of the thick vine cable and swinging *Pegasus* toward the near bank.

"I want to anchor it here," she said, jabbing a finger at the river's edge, "out of the current, so I can get to the vines fouling the engines."

The plan elicited a lively discussion among the men. Like most natives of this part of the Caribbean, they were a handsome people. Their rapid speech rose and fell in a musical rhythm that bespoke their mixture of island and Spanish heritage. After some debate, they agreed Cari's plan would work.

Before any work was done, however, Mac requested two men head back upriver to act as sentries. Just in case someone should come looking for an unidentified river craft. The headman agreed and dispatched two sturdy young villagers in a dugout canoe.

Then it was a matter of waiting while another crew paddled across the river to hack at the far end of the cable. While they paddled, Cari swam back to *Pegasus* and crawled into the cockpit. Mac stayed on shore with a troop of men armed with poles to keep the craft from plowing too hard and too fast into the bank.

Despite her swim, Cari was once again drenched in nervous sweat by the time *Pegasus* was tethered to the shore. She was also squinting to see through the fast-gathering shadows.

"Night drops like a stone this deep in the interior," Harry White warned. "Unless you rig some lights, you'll be working blind in a few minutes."

As little as she liked berthing overnight alongside the river, Cari had to nix the idea of using shipboard batteries to power external lights. "We'll need every ounce of juice to restart the engines. We'll have to wait until morning to unfoul the propellers."

Assuming she *could* unfoul them, that is.

Mac concurred. "It's best not to fumble around underwater in the dark. Lieutenant, why don't you accompany the reverend back to the village, grab some chow and snatch a few hours sleep? I'll use what's left of the netting to camouflage *Pegasus* and take first watch."

He made the suggestion so naturally Cari suspected he didn't even realize he'd assumed command. Since they were once again ashore, she yielded to his authority.

This passing the baton back and forth was becoming a habit with them, she thought wryly. What's more, they were getting pretty good at it, each allowing the other to exercise their unique skills and expertise.

That thought was still in her mind when she made her way back to the river four hours later.

She'd downed a fantastic meal of roast fish, black beans and plantains. She'd also scrubbed away her dirt and sweat, and curled up on a straw mat for three hours of total unconsciousness. Now it was McIver's turn.

She found him stretched out on the bank, back propped against a tree, boots crossed at the ankles, sharing a fire with two of the men from the village. The fire was carefully banked, a mere red glow in the darkness, but it emitted enough smoke to keep the worst of the mosquitoes at bay. Either that, or they shied away from the awful stink put out by the thin, long stemmed pipes clamped between the men's teeth.

"Banana leaves," Mac explained when she dropped down beside him and wrinkled her nose. "Flavored with what I'm guessing is some sort of guano."

"Guano? Like in bird poop?"

"I'm thinking it's more likely bat droppings."

"You're smoking bat droppings?"

His shoulders lifted. "When in Rome…"

This was a whole new side of the man, one Cari

was seeing for the first time. In their months together at the New Mexico test site, she'd pretty well decided his personality and general attitude were every bit as starched as his BDUs. Yet here she was, sitting cross-legged on a riverbank beside him while he smoked bat dung and carried on a lively conversation with two grinning Caribes via grunts and hand signals.

Then there was that kiss.

Now that the tension of the afternoon had eased some of its brutal grip on her mind—and on her neck muscles!—the memory of Mac's mouth coming down hard and hungry on hers kept sneaking into Cari's thoughts. She still couldn't figure out where that kiss had come from, and the fact that she couldn't was driving her nuts.

Unfortunately, she found no opportunity to slip the topic into the conversation. A ferocious rumble from the vicinity of Mac's stomach reminded her he had yet to chow down or get some rest.

"It's my watch," she reminded him. "You'd better go feed that growling beast something other than banana leaves and bat dung."

Mac didn't argue. Like Cari, he'd spent enough years in the field to know the importance of snatching food and rest whenever the situation permitted.

"I'll be back in four hours." Gesturing to his companions to stay and keep her company, he pushed to his feet. "You've got your radio?"

She tapped her shirt pocket. "Right here."

"Contact me if you see anything—anything—that makes you nervous."

"The only thing that worries me at the moment is the possibility these guys might press me to take a turn on your pipe."

In the dim glow from the fire she saw his teeth flash in a quick grin. "You should try a puff or two. It's really not all that bad."

"No, thanks."

He stood for a moment, a dark shadow against the even deeper black of the jungle. "It's been a helluva a day."

"That it has."

Cari couldn't believe she'd jumped out of bed at 5:00 a.m. this morning convinced the most momentous challenge she'd face was taking *Pegasus* into the Gulf of Mexico for his first deep-water swim. Eighteen hours later, she was stranded on a Caribbean island with a boatload of kids, two missionaries and one U.S. Marine.

"You did good today, Lieutenant."

Good grief! Two compliments in one day! Coming from Russ McIver, she was sure that constituted some kind of a world record.

"We both did good," she returned. "Although some people might say I fell a little short of excellence when I hung my boat up on a fishing net."

"Yeah, well, there is that minor problem to rectify. Still…" He hesitated a moment before moving into dangerous territory. "Your friend Jerry might have had his eyes opened if he'd seen you in action today."

She was still formulating her answer to that when another loud rumble cut through the buzz and whir of night insects.

"Go eat something," she insisted.

"Aye, aye, skipper. I'll back in four hours."

He started off, his boots squishing on the spongy vegetation lining the riverbank. Cari debated for all of four or five seconds before unfolding her legs and following after him.

"Hey, McIver!"

"What?"

"You remember that e-mail Captain Westfall suggested we send before departing for Caribe?"

"That isn't something I'm likely to forget in the space of one day."

"I e-mailed Jerry."

She sensed rather than saw his shrug.

"Understandable."

Moving toward him, she wondered why the heck it was suddenly so important to clarify the matter of Commander Jerry Wharton. "Not that it's any of your business, but I turned down his proposal."

Surprise colored his voice. "You did?"

"I did. I also ended things between us."

"Why? Not that it's any of my business."

She hated to surrender ground to a marine, but saw no other choice in this instance. "You were right back in Corpus. I'm good at what I do. Damned good. What's more, I love being part of something important. I ought to be able to find a way to combine a career *and* a family. Other women have certainly managed it."

"You're not other women, Dunn."

The flat assertion left her almost as confused as his kiss had earlier that afternoon. And more than a little irritated. She wasn't sure what kind of reaction she'd been expecting to the news she'd ended things with Jerry, but this certainly wasn't it.

"See you in four hours," she said, turning to make her way back to the two fishermen.

Mac let her go.

He wasn't about to admit her cool announcement had rocked him right back on his boot heels. Nor would he give in to the suddenly fierce urge to grab her wrist, spin her around, and feed the beast inside him that hungered for something other than smoked fish and black beans.

They were on a mission, for God's sake! Responsible for the safety of two Americans and a passel of kids. But when they got the Whites and their charges out of Caribe...

A vivid image leaped into his head. Cari sprawled on a bed. Her hair tangled and dark against white sheets. Her lips swollen. Her brown eyes languorous. Mac went so hard he almost doubled over.

Gritting his teeth, he forced the image out of his head. The vivid detail blurred, but the ache stayed. All these weeks they'd worked together, Mac had refused to let himself think of Caroline Dunn that way, had done his damndest to keep her out of his head. Now he wanted her in his bed so badly he ached with it.

Somehow he suspected he wasn't going to drop off to sleep any time soon.

He had that right.

Stretched out on a raised sleeping platform in the hut given over for the visitors' use, he caught only fitful snatches of sleep. Finally, he dozed off—only to jerk awake again sometime later.

A slow, stealthy rustling in the darkness had him grabbing his assault rifle.

Chapter 5

Rifle to his shoulder, Mac picked out a glowing green figure in the weapon's Night Vision scope.

"Hold it right there!"

His snarled command froze the ghoulish shape in a half crouch. A head whipped around. Eyes surrounded by iridescent green shadows stared at Mac.

Disgusted, he lowered his weapon. "Didn't anyone ever tell you sneaking into a room in the dark of night is a good way to get hurt, kid?"

Evidently not. Paulo scrunched his face into a scowl and looked distinctly unintimidated.

"What are you doing here?" Mac growled. "Why aren't you bedded down with the others?"

As soon as the words were out, he gave himself a mental kick. Oh, that was smart. Why not ask the kid a couple more questions he couldn't respond to? Besides, the answer was obvious now that Mac had shaken the sleep out of his head. The boy was crouched over the webbed utility belt, conducting a little midnight raid.

The possibilities of what he'd find in those pockets made Mac's stomach clench. He'd stuffed a small arsenal of spare ammo clips, grenades and other deadly items in that belt. None of which made suitable toys for children.

Rolling off the woven straw platform, he flicked a match and put it to the wick of the kerosene lamp hanging from a low rafter.

"What are you after?"

At his approach, the kid sprang up and hotfooted it for the straw mat that served as a door. Mac caught him by the collar of his shirt before he could escape.

"Oh, no you don't."

He swung the boy around and faced off with him for the second time that day.

"We need to have a little powwow here, kid. You can't… Ow!"

For a scrawny little runt, the boy sure knew how to put his boney elbows and knees to use. Mac took a sharp whack on the shin that left him feeling distinctly unfriendly.

Paulo gave no signs of feeling any friendlier. With an inarticulate little grunt he twisted around and tried to lock his teeth on a handy patch of wrist. Swearing under his breath, Mac held him at arm's length.

"Now look, pal. Let's get something straight. We're on the same side."

Maybe.

And maybe not.

Now that he thought about it, could be the kid wasn't real anxious to leave Caribe for a new home and as yet unknown adoptive parents in the States. Or could be the boy had an aversion to authority figures. The Lord knew Mac hadn't been on the best of terms with very many in his younger days.

Keeping a firm grip on the ragged Spider-Man shirt, he dragged the sullen boy back over to the belt. "What were you after here? *¿Qué usted, uh, desea?*"

Paulo made an abrupt gesture with one hand. The Whites had taught the boy to communicate via sign language. Mac had never learned signing, but this particular gesture was universally recognizable.

"*¿Que?*" he growled. "Show me."

Scowling, Paulo pointed a grubby finger at the survival knife attached to the belt. The six-inch parkarized steel blade with its serrated top edge and leather-grooved handle lay nestled inside a canvas scabbard.

Mac's eyes narrowed. What the heck did the kid want with a blade like that? The mystery was solved a moment later, when a distracted Harry White came in search of his missing charge.

"There you are! What are you doing?"

Paulo shrugged, leaving Mac to answer. "From what I can gather, he came after my knife."

"Oh, dear."

White directed a torrent of Caribe at the boy, who answered with a flurry of hand signals.

"He didn't want the knife," the minister interpreted. "Just the sheath. Show him, Paulo."

With a fierce scowl, the boy dug his hand into the pocket of his shorts. When he withdrew it, his grubby fist was clenched tight. It took a gentle prod from the missionary to get him to uncurl his fingers.

In his palm lay a small pocketknife. The handle must have been inlaid with mother-of-pearl at one time, but most of the iridescent shell had chipped away. Shooting Mac an evil look, Paulo dug out the blade. The steel was broken off at the tip and rusted in spots, but it was clear the knife was the boy's prize possession. It was also clear why he'd wanted the sheath of Mac's survival knife. Hunkering down, the boy drew the broken blade along the narrow whetstone sewn into the side seam of the canvas scabbard. For a moment the snick of steel against flint was the only sound in the hut.

"The knife was in his pocket when he showed up at the back door of the mission," White explained while Paulo methodically sharpened the blade. "He was only four or five at the time. Far too young for such an implement, of course, but every time we took the thing away and hid it, he'd ferret it out. We've since discovered he's very careful with it. And quite good at carving beads and toys for the other children from seed pods and monkey wood."

Mac would bet the little tough could probably carve his initials in a man's shinbone, too. He kept his thoughts to himself and expression neutral, though, until the boy had whetted the blade to his satisfaction. Rising, he snapped the blade shut, dropped the knife in his pocket and started to saunter off.

"Paulo!"

White said something in Caribe. The boy's lips pressed tight. His jaw jutted.

Sighing, the minister tried again. "The major let you use his whetstone. What do you say?"

At the gentle suggestion, the youngster flashed a quick hand signal. The tips of the missionary's ears turned a bright pink.

"He, er, said thank you."

Yeah, Mac just bet he did.

Quickly, White shooed the boy into the other room. His ears still glowing, he spread his hands apologetically. "Paulo has had a rough time. From the little we've been able to pry out of him, he apparently saw his mother murdered by the rebels, along with half of his village.''

So it wasn't just anyone in authority the kid reacted so strongly to. It was anyone in BDUs. Feeling a tug of pity for a child who'd taken some major hits in his six short years, Mac asked about his father.

''We don't know who he was or what happened to him. Paulo just showed up at the mission one day. No one in the government bureaucracy can produce so much as a birth certificate or baptismal record for him. It's pretty much the same story with all the kids. That's why we've had such a difficult time getting them out of Caribe. They have no papers, therefore they don't exist.''

Remembering his earlier thought, Mac posed another question. ''Are you so sure they want to leave Caribe? It's their home.''

''We're sure. They know they're going to families who've waited for years to adopt. All except Paulo. We've had some difficulty placing him, but finally found a family who's willing to take him after he completes his surgery.''

''What surgery?''

''My sister's been in contact with doctors at the M.D. Anderson Cancer Center in Houston. They've experienced considerable success implanting artificial voice boxes in patients with severe throat cancer. It would take a number of delicate operations, but we're hoping they can do the same for Paulo.''

The thought of the scruffy kid in the next room going under the knife for a series of operations left Mac feeling distinctly uncomfortable. So much so, he couldn't get back to sleep after Reverend White returned to the other room. Edgy and restless, he hooked his utility belt over one shoulder, jammed on his hat and slipped out of the hut.

He used his pencil-thin high-intensity flashlight to find his way to the river. All around him, the jungle was alive with the sights and sounds. Night-feeding creatures crunched on leaves and insects. Bats whooshed through the trees. A dozen or more red dots glowed in the inky blackness, steady, unblinking eyes that followed Mac's passage.

The carefully banked fire was little more than an orange blush in the darkness, but provided enough light for Mac to observe the trio keeping *Pegasus* company. Cari had assumed the same comfortable position Mac had earlier—her back against a peeling banyan trunk, legs crossed at the ankles. She'd evidently declined their hosts' offer of a pipe, however. The two Caribe fishermen squatted comfortably nearby, providing more than enough pungent smoke to keep the mosquitoes away without her assistance.

"It's McIver," Mac called out in a quiet voice so as not to startle them too much. "I'm coming in."

Cari sat up, chiding herself for the ridiculous way her pulse skittered at the sound of his voice. How like McIver to materialize out of the night just when her wayward thoughts had returned to him…for only the ninth or tenth time in the past few hours!

She darted a quick look at the illuminated face of her watch, confirmed it *was* only a few hours since she'd relieved him. "What are you doing back here?" Her voice sharpened. "Is there a problem?"

"No problem. I just couldn't sleep."

Nodding to the two fishermen, Mac folded his legs and made himself comfortable beside her. She scooted over a few inches to give him a share of the tree to lean against. The other men seemed to take his arrival as a signal for them to abandon their post. In a mix of Spanish, Caribe and eloquent hand gestures, they indicated it was time for them to hit the rack and melted into the jungle.

A minute ago, the muted symphony of night sounds and mostly incomprehensible murmur of her two self-appointed guardians had lulled Cari into a relaxed, sleepy state. All of a sudden she was wide-awake, her every nerve tingling. Deciding some conversation would force her mind away from Mac's close proximity, she angled her face toward his.

"Why couldn't you sleep?"

''I kept thinking about that e-mail you sent Wharton.''

''What about it?'' she asked, surprised and just a little wary.

He hesitated a moment or two before making a grudging admission. ''Maybe I was out of line, pushing at you the way I did back in Corpus.''

''Maybe?''

''Okay, I tend to come on a little strong at times. The point is, I shouldn't have ragged you. Not about something so important. And maybe you shouldn't have given Wharton his walking papers. That isn't the kind of decision a person should make right before taking off on a mission.''

The comment took Cari completely aback. After the bone-rattling kiss that afternoon, she would have supposed he'd be the last one to suggest she'd made a mistake with Jerry.

Or maybe this was his way of suggesting *he'd* made a mistake, she thought with a sudden lurch in her belly. Maybe he was worried she'd read too much into a simple lip-lock.

''I knew what I was doing,'' she said coolly. ''*Not* that it's any of your business.''

''You tried that line already. It didn't work the first time.''

''What is this?'' she asked, confused and beginning

to feel a little annoyed. "When did my personal life become a matter of such interest to you?"

"Since the first time I laid eyes on you back in New Mexico."

He dropped that bombshell so calmly, so casually, that it took a few seconds for the full impact to hit.

"Are you saying you've...you've..."

She stumbled, not quite sure how to phrase matters at this point. Mac supplied the missing link.

"Had the hots for you since day one? As a matter of fact, I have."

Her jaw dropped. Several scenes from the past months flashed into her mind. In most of them, she and Russ McIver had been squaring off for another round.

He must have sensed her shock. She saw the ghost of a grin sketch across his face.

"I know. It's kind of knocked me off my stride, too."

"Ha!" That at least she could respond to. "If I knocked you off stride any time in the past four months, you sure as heck hid it well."

"Every time I was ready to make my move, you'd get another call from Wharton. I saw the pressure those calls put on you. I wasn't going to add to it."

Cari had no idea Mac had observed her so closely. Or pegged her uncertainty over her relationship with Jerry so accurately. More confused than ever, she pushed away from the tree trunk, sat up straight and tried to see his face in the gloom.

"You didn't hesitate to add some pressure this afternoon," she reminded him pointedly. "You didn't know I'd ended things with Jerry when you laid that kiss on me."

"No, I didn't. We can chalk that one up to galloping adrenaline."

That was pretty much what Cari had figured. Still, hearing Mac confirm it put a decided dent in her ego. Before she could formulate an appropriate response, however, he reached over and curved a palm around her nape.

"This one," he said as he tugged her closer, "is for real."

It was. Most definitely. For real.

His mouth came down on hers, not as hard as it had that afternoon, but every bit as hungry. Surprise held Cari stiff-shouldered for a moment. Only for a moment. Then his lips moved over hers and hunger spiked through her.

She wanted more than a taste this time. She wanted teeth and tongue. A little full-frontal contact would be nice, too, she decided on a rush of heat. Twisting sideways, she wrapped her arms around his neck. The move brought their upper bodies into play, but left the lower portions at an awkward angle. Mac solved the problem by snaking his other arm around her waist and hauling her across his lap.

"There," he murmured against her mouth. "That's better."

"Much better."

Her agreement began on a breathy laugh and ended on a gulp. She was still at an angle, but wouldn't complain about the amount of contact now. She could feel his thighs under hers, his ribs against her breast, the bristly hair on the back of his neck beneath her palm. His front was bristly, too, she discovered when his cheeks and chin rasped against hers.

"This isn't real smart," she gasped after she came up for air.

"Not smart at all," Mac agreed, nuzzling her throat. "Want me to stop?"

His teeth scraped a path along the tender skin, his tongue ignited a trail of fire.

"Later," she got out on a breathless gasp.

Much later.

First she wanted to feel his hands on her, wanted *her* hands on him…without several layers of chemically treated jungle BDUs between them. She fumbled with the buttons on his shirt, shoved the flaps aside, ran her palms over the planes and curves covered by a wide expanse of black cotton T-shirt.

Mac did the same, except he made shorter work of her buttons and didn't stop with her T-shirt. One swift yank pulled up the hem, exposing her sports bra. Another tug brought the springy spandex lower, baring the slopes of her breasts. They were on the small side, like the rest of her, but provided more than enough material for Mac's busy, busy hands and mouth to work with.

His breath came through the spandex, hot and wet. His teeth found the tight, eager nipple pushing against the elastic. Within moments, fire was shooting from Cari's breast straight to her belly. Moments more, and she was squirming frantically on his lap.

"Oh, babe," he half muttered, half groaned. "Another move like that and it will be *too* late."

"Huh?"

Lost to the sensations piling one on top of the other, Cari struggled to put the skids on her whirling senses. It took a hard, insistent probe at her left rear cheek to penetrate her sensual haze.

"Oh. Right."

Tugging down her bra, she wiggled off his lap. She heard a long, low hiss, followed by a sound that could only be teeth grinding.

"Wrong time, wrong place," she said with a shaky laugh. She was pushing the buttons of her shirt through their holes when Mac curled a knuckle under her chin and tipped her face to his.

"There'll be a right time," he promised gruffly. "And a right place."

''Will there?''

''Damn straight.''

Now that some semblance of sanity had returned, Cari wasn't so sure. With any luck, they'd depart Caribe and hit the open sea by noon. After that, it was only a matter of weeks—maybe days—until the Pegasus test cadre disbanded. When that happened, she'd go back to her home station in Maryland and Mac would return to the marine corps base at Cherry Point, North Carolina.

The thought depressed her. More, she realized with a small shock, than her abrupt decision to terminate her yearlong relationship with Jerry Wharton.

Whoa! How the heck had she let things get so heavy, so fast? She'd just opted out of one relationship that had presented insurmountable challenges. She had to be crazy to even *think* about jumping out of that situation into one involving a gung ho marine. Particularly a marine who held very definite opinions on just about everything and didn't hesitate to express them.

Torn between regret and relief that they'd stopped when they had, Cari shoved the last button through its hole and tucked her shirt inside her waistband to keep out the mosquitoes. A quick glance at her watch provided an excuse to put some distance between her and Mac and let the dust settle a bit.

''It's almost four. You sure you don't want to go

back to the village and grab another hour or two of sleep?''

''I'm sure.''

The dry response told Cari he was still wound as tight as she was. Neither one of them were likely to uncoil in the remaining hours before dawn.

''Then I'll head back and round up a work crew as soon as it turns light. With the help of some strong backs and sharp machetes, we'll soon have *Pegasus* back in trim.''

Or so she hoped.

Chapter 6

Seven hours later, Cari stood on the bank of the Rio Verde while Janice White doctored a deep, slicing cut in the web of skin between her thumb and forefinger. Wet hair straggled in long tangles around her face and shoulders. River water slicked down her face and plastered her pants to her body. She'd discarded her BDU shirt but a large, boisterous crowd of observers had prevented her from stripping down to her bra.

Shaking her head, she surveyed the scene of what had begun as a recovery operation and now looked more like a three-ring circus. Dugout canoes were strung across the river, filled with Caribes calling out advice and beating the surface with sticks to keep away any unwanted underwater creatures. Women squatted on the bank, laughing and chatting and offering their own opinions on the operation. Shrieking children cannonballed through the ferns into the river and sent up sparkling geysers. With the quicksilver agility of minnows, they darted around the craft Cari and Mac had yet to free from the last remnants of the fishing net.

The Whites and their charges had joined the throng who'd turned out to observe the recovery operation. Rosa, the bright-eyed little girl with the twisted spine, sat cross-legged next to the boy with the cleft palate. Together they described events for Miguel, whose sightless eyes couldn't see what was happening. Paulo stood a little apart from the others. His face was set in its habitual scowl as he glared at the marine treading water at *Pegasus*'s stern.

Like Cari, Mac had discarded his fatigue shirt. He'd also stripped off his black cotton T-shirt. Water glistened on his bare shoulders and arms as he waited for Janice White to finish treating Cari's cut.

His lip curling, Paulo looked from the marine to Cari. When he whipped up his hands and signed a message, Janice White interpreted.

"Paulo says the major has big paws."

No kidding! Having experienced the movement of those paws over strategic points of her body just last night, Cari could vouch for their size.

"*Too* big, Paulo says."

For their current task, anyway. She and Mac had already conceded that point.

After determined hacking, they'd cut through the larger vines and cleared away most of the obstruction. Now they were down to the small, fibrous tentacles caught in the threads of the engines. It was painstaking work, done under water in murky light with only the pencil-thin flashlights to guide them. Mac was now relegated to holding the light while Cari's smaller, more nimble fingers probed the sharp blades and screws. The *very* sharp blades and screws.

Another cut like this one and she'd start worrying about piranha being drawn by the blood. The hastily thrown together briefing she and Mac had received on Caribe's riverine conditions hadn't indicated any native man-eating species besides crocs, which the villagers were keeping a sharp eye out for. But then their pre-mission brief hadn't included the fact that the Whites were brother and sister, either. Cari wasn't particularly anxious to discover another gap in their intelligence.

A flash of hands to her left drew her gaze.

"Paulo says his fingers are smaller," Janice duly reported. "He wants to help."

Without waiting for a go-ahead, the boy reached into the pocket of his shorts and dug out a pocketknife. Flipping open the blade, he plunged into the river.

"No, wait!"

Cari's protest was lost in a loud splash. Paulo went under, bobbed up again a few yards away from the stern, and tossed his head to get the water out of his eyes. His mouth set, he paddled toward Mac and the half-submerged craft.

"He'll hurt himself," Cari said worriedly, trying to yank her hand free.

Dr. White kept it in a firm grasp. "The boy is remarkably handy with that knife. Perhaps he can help."

Turning a six-year-old armed with a rusty pocketknife loose on a multimillion-dollar test vehicle wasn't Cari's idea of smart. Mac obviously shared her concerns. As Paulo shot underwater, the marine kicked up his boot heels and went after him.

Her cut bandaged, Cari was at the bank ready to dive in when Mac popped back up. Paulo followed a moment later. Raising a fist, he displayed a long, stringlike trophy.

Mac acknowledged his accomplishment with a grin. Reaching over, he knuckled the boy on the head. "Good job, kid."

An answering grin split Paulo's face. It only lasted a moment or two, but for those moments a smug, happy child replaced the sullen boy.

"Want to give it another shot?"

Nodding, Paulo tossed the stringy vine into the swirling current, jackknifed, and disappeared under the surface once again. Mac up-ended, scissor-kicked and followed. Still worried that the boy would hurt himself and/or her craft, Cari dived in as well.

It took a dozen more dives before they cleared the twin propellers of all foreign objects. By then Mac's chest heaved and Cari had to pull in deep, ragged breaths each time they surfaced. Paulo, on the other hand, appeared to have a child's inexhaustible source of energy. Popping in and out of the water like a playful seal pup, he swam circles around Cari and Mac as they prepared to board *Pegasus*.

"Better wait on the bank," Mac advised his young helper. "We need you and everyone else to stay clear while we fire up the engines."

If they fired them up, Cari thought grimly. Praying she hadn't stripped the gears or bent the blades when she plowed through the net, she grabbed an edge of the open cockpit to haul herself up. Mac planted a hand on her rear and gave her an added boost.

"Thanks," she drawled, scrambling over the edge.

With a flex of water-slick muscles, he pulled himself up after her. He looked like a pirate rising out of the sea to board a captured vessel, Cari thought. Dark bristles shadowed his cheeks and chin. Water sluiced down his bare chest. His mottled green-and-black pants hung low on his hips. All he needed was a cutlass thrust through his belt to complete the image. Forcing her gaze from that expanse of naked chest, she settled into her seat.

"We'd better advise Captain Westfall that we're going to attempt to power up. Why don't you take care of that while I run the preignition checklist?"

"Will do."

Cupping his hands, he called to Harry White to toss him his handheld radio. The instrument came sailing through the air. Moments later, Mac had a link to the navy captain.

They'd been providing Westfall periodic updates of their situation. He'd called in a Pavehawk helicopter as backup and was fully prepared to launch another expedition to extract both the Pegasus crew and their passengers. If she couldn't power up her craft, Cari thought, that's what it would come to.

Hating the thought of abandoning *Pegasus* deep in the Caribe jungle, she checked the gauge on the auxiliary power source. They had barely enough juice left for ignition. Once the engines were running, they could recharge the batteries and power up the navigational systems.

"Here goes," she muttered to Mac.

Her finger hovered over the auxiliary power switch for a moment before flicking it on. The gauge's needle shivered, whipped from red to green, danced back to yellow. When Cari pressed the switch to fire the starboard engine, the needle zinged into the red again.

"Come on, baby."

She lifted her thumb, pressed the switch again. The needle stayed glued to the red. Her stomach was tying itself into knots when the engine gave a low growl. Slowly, the props began to churn.

"Yes!"

The watchers on the bank sent up a round of shouts and cheers. Cari barely heard them as she quickly throttled the starboard engine to Neutral and hit the switch for the port side engine. The needle on the auxiliary power gauge jerked once, a pathetic little bob, then lay flat. But there was enough juice, *just* enough, to ignite the second engine.

The propellers began to turn, raising another chorus of whoops and cheers. This time Cari acknowledged them. Keeping a careful hand on the throttle, she waved wildly with the other. A wide grin split her face when she turned to Mac.

"Well, whaddya know! Looks like we might not have to leave *Pegasus* behind, after all."

"Looks like." His hazel eyes glinting, he keyed his radio. "Pegasus Base, this is Pegasus One. We've powered up both engines."

"That's good to hear, One."

Westfall didn't try to disguise his relief. This supersecret vehicle was his baby, his project, but he would have ordered Cari and Mac to abandon it in a heartbeat if faced with undue risk. Thankfully, that hadn't proved to be the case. So far.

"The engineers indicate it'll take ninety minutes to fully recharge the batteries and power up all systems," the captain advised. "How's your fuel?"

Cari gave Mac a thumbs-up.

"We should have enough to bring us home," he relayed.

"We'll be standing by," Westfall replied tersely. "Just in case."

The whole Pegasus team would be standing with him, Cari knew. Jill. Doc. Kate. Dave Scott. She could count on any or all of them to charge to the rescue.

That's what separated the military from civilian institutions, she acknowledged silently. This unspoken bond, this brotherhood of arms. She'd become part of that brotherhood the first time she'd raised her hand and sworn to protect and defend. After all these years, the military was in her blood. Had she really thought she could give it up? Did she *have* to give it up to have a family?

Her heart said no, but the stubborn little voice of practicality inside her head wanted to know just how the heck she thought she could raise children and take off at a moment's notice on missions like this one.

Shoving that question aside to be addressed later, Cari concentrated on the task at hand—recharging *Pegasus*'s batteries.

"You'd better tell the Whites we'll be ready to depart in ninety minutes," she said to Mac. "I'll watch the power levels and bring up our onboard systems one by one."

Nodding, Mac made the transition from ship to shore. After a brief consultation, the Whites decided to shepherd their charges back to the village to gather their few belongings and down a quick meal. Mac lifted the bright, chattering Rosa to her customary riding place on Reverend White's shoulders. Janice White took Miguel's hand firmly in hers to lead him along the narrow jungle path. Paulo carried a younger child piggyback and got another knuckle-rub from Mac as he passed. The boy hunched his shoulders and shied away, but his scowl lacked some of its usual ferocity.

Since the show appeared to be pretty well over, the rest of the women and children trailed along after the Whites. Even the men brought their canoes to shore and made for the cluster of huts.

"We need to come up with a gift for the villagers," Mac said when he rejoined Cari in the open cockpit. "Something to thank them for their hospitality."

"I've been thinking about that, too. *Pegasus* is designed to carry troops or cargo pallets. There are several rolls of cargo webbing stowed in the rear compartment. The webbing is super-lightweight nylon and almost indestructible. A roll of that stuff would make an excellent replacement for the fishing net we chewed up.''

''So it would. Good thinking, Dunn. I'll dig a roll out of the hold.'' He clambered out of his seat, but paused as an amber light began to blink on the instrument panel. ''Is that the Marine Navigational System?''

''It is!''

With a quick jab of relief, Cari watched the MNS display screen come to life. The dull gray of the screen faded and was replaced by a digitized map of Caribe. A long, squiggly line represented the Rio Verde. The amber dot, now a steady glow, indicated their current position.

Mac clapped a hand on her shoulder and gave it a squeeze. ''Looks like we're back in business.''

''Almost.''

To Cari's consternation, the clean, sharp scent of river-washed male cut right through her elation at getting the navigational system up. Her concentration took another hit when Mac leaned over her shoulder to peer at the checklist in her lap.

''What's next?''

Oh, sure! Like she could read a checklist with

McIver's wet, naked chest snuggled against her cheek?

"Next up are, uh, the defensive systems."

"Be good to get our eyes and ears back on line," he commented, pushing upright. "It makes me feel real goosey having only a couple sentries out there between us and the bad guys."

It made Cari feel goosey, too. Almost as goosey as the final squeeze Mac gave her shoulder before sliding open the panel to the rear compartment. The ripple effect of that casual caress went all the way down to her toes.

For Pete's sake! What the heck was going on with her? One short, hot session in Mac's arms and she approached total meltdown if he so much as looked sideways at her.

Exasperated, Cari shook her head. So much for her decision to back off and let the embers stirred by one man die before jumping into the fire with another. In two short days Major Russ McIver had crowded Commander Jerry Wharton right out of her head.

How long he would stay there after the Pegasus cadre disbanded had yet to be determined, Cari reminded herself.

Well, what would happen, would happen. Right now her focus had to be getting *Pegasus* ready to swim again.

* * *

She had half of the systems powered up and was tapping her fingers impatiently on the checklist when Mac called from the rear compartment.

"Hey, Dunn!"

"What?"

"Thought you might want to know the environmental systems are fully operational. It's downright chilly back here."

"No kidding?"

The prospect of even a few minutes relief from the suffocating jungle heat was too tempting to resist. Cari checked the instrument panel, estimated it would take another twelve minutes for the hydraulic system to achieve maximum efficiency, and tossed the checklist onto the seat next to hers. Mere seconds later, she was leaning against the sliding door separating the cabin from the cockpit, bathed in blessedly cool air.

"Ahhhhh."

Mac flashed a grin. "Feels good, doesn't it?"

"*Good* doesn't begin to describe it."

She closed her eyes, letting the heat and suffocating humidity leach from her bones. The climate-controlled air felt so wonderful she didn't notice when her sopping BDU pants and T-shirt went from merely wet to downright clammy.

Mac did, however. "You've got goose bumps popping out up and down your arms."

She waved a careless hand. "What are a few goose bumps compared to such bliss?"

"My T-shirt's dry." Scooping up the wad of black cotton, he tossed it in her direction. "You're welcome to change into it."

It was more than just dry, Cari discovered after snagging the garment midair. It was soft and warm and carried the scent of sun. Not to mention a distinctive blend of raw masculinity that was all Mac.

Dropping it on the webbed seat, she dragged up the hem of her wet shirt. She'd bared two inches of midriff before she noticed that McIver had crossed his arms and propped his shoulders against the bulkhead.

"I take it you're just going to stand there and enjoy the show?"

His eyes glinted. "That's the plan."

"Hmm."

Pursing her lips, Cari debated whether to perform for her one-person audience. She certainly hadn't had any reservations last night. She'd come within a breath of stripping to her skin. Okay, she'd pretty well *ached* to shed every scrap of clothing she had on.

As hot and heavy as those moments had been, though, there was something infinitely more disconcerting about peeling off a wet T-shirt in the bright light of day, with Mac's very intent, very interested gaze aimed in her direction. Which was crazy, since that same wet T-shirt made it obvious she was wearing another garment under the cotton.

Crazy or not, Cari's skin prickled from more than the cool air as she raised her arms and dragged the damp, clingy cotton over her head. Common sense told her to grab Mac's shirt and pull it on. A perverse, wholly feminine instinct told her to take her time.

Casually, she tugged at the lower hem of her bra to adjust the wet spandex. The fabric stretched taut over the tips of her breasts, which had gone tight and stiff in reaction to the cool air. To Cari's intense satisfaction, Mac's breath left on a little hiss.

Shoving away from the bulkhead, he stepped over the roll of cargo netting he'd retrieved from the storage compartment. His voice held a rough edge but his touch was tender as he drew a knuckle down the slopes of her breasts.

"Do you have any idea how gorgeous you are?"

She hadn't looked into a mirror in going on thirty-six hours and would probably shriek when she did. She wasn't about to argue with the man, however.

"You aren't so bad yourself, big guy."

"You're just saying that because you've got a thing for buzz cuts and sidewalls."

Buzz cuts and sidewalls and little white squint lines at the corners of sexy hazel eyes, Cari admitted silently. Not to mention a strong, square chin and a set of pecs right out of *Bench Press Quarterly*. Tiny shivers rippled along the surface of her skin as his knuckle traced a path down the slope of her other breast.

After the frenzied urgency of last night, this slow, soft caress was incredibly arousing. She stood still under the whisper-light stroke as long as she could before giving in to the need to touch him.

Gliding her fingertips across his chest, she imprinted every sensation. The damp heat rising under her fingers. The smooth bulge of skin and muscle. The dusting of dark hair arrowing down to his waist. She kept her touch every bit as light as Mac's, yet her breath was soon coming as fast and rough as his.

She should have known touching wouldn't be enough—for either of them. Her pulse pounding, Cari tipped her head back and opened her mouth eagerly under his. One kiss and they'd picked up right where they'd left off last night. She clung to him, every nerve in her body singing.

The rush of blood was so swift and fast she almost missed the echo of a distant shout. Mac caught the sound, though. Jerking his head up, he listened intently for a moment before thrusting her away.

"Get dressed."

She was already grabbing at the dry T-shirt. Yanking it over her head, she clambered into the open cockpit after Mac. The sight of two men paddling furiously downriver in their direction started a curl of dread in her stomach. Something had obviously alarmed the sentries.

It alarmed her, too, when they relayed their news using a mix of English, Spanish, and Caribe.

"Boat comes. Big boat. With gun."

The sentry held two fists waist high, as if gripping handles, and stuttered like a machine gun.

"Sounds like a patrol boat," Cari forced out through a suddenly dry throat.

"They come slow," the other fisherman put in. "Stop many times. Search bank."

"How far away?" Mac asked urgently.

"Three bends of river."

Cari drew a map in her head of the snaking Rio Verde and came up with a rough guesstimate.

"I make that a half hour. Maybe more if the boat is moving as slowly as they say."

Her mind racing, she weighed their options. They could abandon *Pegasus* and fade into the jungle with the Whites and the kids. Or they could make a run for it.

"How long before you can get us underway?" Mac snapped, breaking into her thoughts.

"We're barely halfway through the sequence of powering up the onboard systems."

"How long?"

Desperately, she drew on the months she'd spent

The Right Stuff

prepping for *Pegasus*'s water trials. "Ten minutes, if we stay on surface. Twenty, if we want to go below."

Mac didn't hesitate. He was as determined as Cari not to leave their craft behind.

"We'll go surface." Scooping up the roll of cargo webbing, he headed for the cockpit. "I'll get the Whites and the kids. I'll also see if I can convince our hosts to rig another fishnet, like fast. With any luck, they'll snag the patrol boat the same way they did *Pegasus* and buy us a little more time."

Chapter 7

Cari raced through the checklist and brought up only the absolute essential systems. The last to come alive was the Satellite Surveillance System, which picked up the infrared heat signature of a watercraft some miles upriver and displayed it in the form of a faint amber dot. The signal was weak due the satellite's inability to fully penetrate the dense jungle canopy, but strong enough to confirm the craft was in fact a patrol boat—heavily armed and moving slowly, but definitely heading in their direction.

Keeping one eye on that amber dot, Cari had the engines revving and *Pegasus* ready to shake free of the mooring lines when Mac came charging out of the jungle with Rosa on his shoulders. The two missionaries and the rest of the children scrambled after him. In their wake came most of the village.

While Mac handed the Whites and the kids aboard, the local men made for their canoes. Cari had time for only a few shouted words of thanks and a wild wave before Mac freed the mooring lines. As soon as he'd jumped into the cockpit, she closed the canopy, steered her craft out to midchannel and throttled up. To her infinite relief, the twin, rear-tilted engines gave a throaty roar. Their propellers cut into the water. With the delta-shaped wings acting like a hydrofoil, *Pegasus* raised his nose out of the water, sprayed a long silver arc behind him, and sped downriver.

Cari kept her eyes on the instruments and her hands fisted on the controls. "You'd better get on the horn and inform base of the situation. See if they can get the particulars on that patrol boat."

They could and did. Captain Westfall came back on the radio within moments with the information that rebels had seized the boat two days earlier from government forces, killing all aboard. He also confirmed that it was heavily armed.

"Be advised that we'll have a Pavehawk in the air within the next ten minutes," Westfall said tersely. "The chopper will be waiting for you when you exit the mouth of the river and fly cover while you cross the open sea."

That was welcome news. *Very* welcome news. A highly modified version of the army's Blackhawk helicopter, the Pavehawk had enough firepower to hold off a dozen patrol boats. Now all Cari had to do was get her craft and her passengers to the mouth of the Rio Verde.

Her heart in her throat, she put on as much speed as she dared given the river's sharp twists and turns. At the same time, she gauged the progress of the glowing amber dot trailing them.

Mac, too, kept his jaw locked and his eyes on the display screen. He gave a muttered curse when the patrol picked up speed and inched closer, an exclamation of relief when it suddenly stopped dead.

"Yes!"

Cari tore her gaze from the green river ahead to take a fix on the boat's location. "Looks like they're at about the same spot where we hit."

"Looks like."

"Think they're caught?"

"Either that or they spotted the cargo webbing and decided to stop and investigate."

"I hope the villagers don't take heat for helping us."

Mac shook his head. "They won't. The headman told me he and his people would melt into the jungle at the first sound of an engine. How far to the coast?"

Her glance dipped to the instruments. "Three miles

as the crow flies. Forever, the way the river snakes back on itself at every turn.''

''Just keep us heading in the right direction and… Hell!''

The terse expletive sent Cari's hope that they'd make a clean escape plunging straight to the river bottom. Her jaw tight, she watched the amber dot begin to move again.

''They must have cut through the webbing,'' Mac muttered. ''They're picking up speed.''

''I see.'' She dragged in a deep breath. ''Go back and make sure our passengers are strapped in. I'm going to open it up.''

The next twenty minutes were the longest of Cari's life. Her heart pounded out every second, every bend they rounded, every centimeter the patrol boat nudged closer. They were still a long, twisting half mile from the mouth of the river when Mac bit out a terse command.

''Pop the canopy.''

''What?''

''Throttle back and pop the canopy.''

She tore her gaze from the green-shrouded river and saw he'd snapped the ammo clip out of his assault rifle. He checked the rounds and shoved the clip back in before meeting her slicing frown.

"They're closing too fast," he said grimly. "I'll have to slow them down."

"Mac, no!"

"It's our only chance." He jerked his chin toward the rear compartment. "Those kids' only chance. I'll stir up a little rear-action diversion, then hotfoot it downriver. The Pavehawk can pick me up."

"I don't like this."

"Throttle back, Cari."

She shot a look at the amber dot, snarled a vicious curse, and pulled back on the controls. Mere seconds after the canopy lifted, Mac splashed into the river. She saw him go under, bob to the surface, kick for shore. Then she shoved the throttle forward and sent *Pegasus* racing around another bend.

Her chest squeezing, she divided her attention between the twisting waterway ahead and the small screen. The patrol boat was less than a hundred meters behind and coming on fast. When it took that last bend, its crew would have her in their gun sites.

"Okay, Mac. If you're gonna do it, you'll have to do it now."

She gripped the wheel, prepared to take evasive action, when the patrol boat swerved wildly, took a sharp turn, and doubled back.

The roar of her craft's engines swallowed all other sounds. Cari had no idea whether Mac had opened fire, couldn't tell if the rebels were returning it. Every instinct screamed at her to go back, to employ *Pegasus*'s not inconsiderable firepower as cover for Mac. Only the safety of the passengers she'd been sent in to rescue kept her on course.

By the time she rounded a final bend and caught a shimmer of blue far ahead, her jaw had locked tight. She'd also come to an unshakable decision. She was damned if she'd leave Mac to fight a rearguard action through a half mile of jungle.

The Pavehawk couldn't go in for him. The dense canopy was too thick for the chopper to penetrate. So Cari would transfer her passengers to the helo and go back herself. Snatching up her radio, she contacted the HH-60.

"This is Pegasus One. Be advised I'm approaching the mouth of the river. Request you set down on the beach immediately and prepare to receive passengers."

The reply was swift and unquestioning. "Roger, Pegasus One. Setting down now."

The river widened. Green water merged with indigo, eddied into sapphire. Tangled vines and giant ferns gave way to a fringe of palms and a snowy-white beach. *Pegasus* shot out of the darkness of the jungle into a light so dazzling Cari had to throw up an arm to shield her eyes.

She spotted the chopper mere yards away, its huge blades churning up a vortex of sand as it settled onto the beach. Spinning the wheel, she cut through the rolling surf, hit the switch to open the belly and lower the wide-track wheels. A moment later, *Pegasus* churned to a stop just outside the reach of the chopper's whirling blades.

The Pavehawk's side hatch opened. A half-dozen uniformed figures jumped out and ducked under the whirling blades. They included, Cari saw with a jolt of surprise, most of the Pegasus cadre.

There was no mistaking Kate Hargrave's flaming auburn hair or Jill Bradshaw's distinctive black armband with the initials ''MP'' emblazoned in big yellow letters. Doc Richardson charged across the sand behind the two women with Dave Scott at his heels. Cari caught a glimpse of Captain Westfall's tall, spare figure as she popped her seat harness and scrambled into the rear compartment.

''We've got a chopper all ready to ferry you and the children out of Caribe,'' she informed the anxious Whites. ''Let's get you transferred.''

The moment Cari opened the hatch, her friends were all there to help with the transfer. Kate took little Tomas. Doc Richardson hefted a wide-eyed Rosa in his arms. Dave Scott hustled Paulo to the Pavehawk, where the boy dug in his heels and refused to climb aboard. His chin set at a stubborn angle, he signed an urgent demand.

"He wants to know where the major is," a harried Janice White interpreted.

"Tell him the major will rejoin him at the base," Dave said.

"He's mute, not deaf," Cari explained as she passed one of the youngsters to the Pavehawk's load-master. "Dr. White, you'd better take a head count."

Nodding, the missionary poked her head inside the chopper and conducted a swift inventory. "...seven, eight, nine with Paulo here. We're all here."

"See you back at base."

Cari spun away, her mind already on the journey back up river. An insistent tug on her fatigue shirt brought her back around.

"Paulo, I've got to go!"

The boy hung on to her fiercely with one hand while he dug his other into the pocket of his shorts. When he produced his rusted pocketknife, Cari looked at him blankly.

"You want me to take your knife?"

Jerking his chin in a quick affirmative, he shoved it into her hand and signed another urgent message.

"He says you might need it," Janice White trans-lated. "To cut the major's ropes if the rebels have him."

Her throat tight, Cari closed her fingers over the small implement. If the rebels had taken Mac alive, she'd need more than a pocketknife to free him. But the fact that this child was willing to part with his only possession to aid in that effort made her throat go tight.

"Thank you," she said gruffly. "I'll return it to you when we get back to base."

Clutching the knife in a tight fist, she raced back to *Pegasus*. The rest of the cadre was already aboard. Jill. Kate. Doc. Dave. Even Sam Westfall. The captain wasn't about to leave one of his own behind. With Dave Scott strapped into the copilot's seat beside her, Cari took the multimillion-dollar craft back up the river.

The rebels hadn't captured Mac. As the tense recovery team discovered when *Pegasus* careened around the second bend in the river, he was still fighting a fierce rearguard action.

Cari's heart leaped into her throat when she spotted tracers from the patrol boat's bow-mounted machine arc from ship to shore. Vegetation flew into the air, shredded by the vicious stream of bullets.

"They're hunting someone," Dave Scott bit out as he searched the bank with high-powered goggles. "Has to be Russ."

Sure enough, an answering stream of gunfire ripped through the ferns lining the bank some distance ahead of the patrol boat. The short burst cut in front of its prow and threw up a high curtain of water. The shielding spray gave Cari the few precious seconds she needed to activate *Pegasus*'s offensive fire systems.

She ached to launch a missile. Just one! The sophisticated, laser-guided rocket would blow the patrol boat out of the water. Unfortunately, their orders were to get in and out of Caribe without engaging either government or rebel troops unless under extreme duress. The fact that Mac had directed his fire in front of the boat's prow indicated he, too, was trying to adhere to the rules of engagement by creating a diversion and not taking out the boat or its crew.

Good thing *Pegasus* came equipped with a few surprises besides precision-guided missiles. Keying her mike, Cari barked out an update for the folks in the rear compartment.

"We have the patrol boat in sight. Hang tight. I'm going to launch a smoker."

Before the words were out of her mouth, she jammed her thumb on the button. The small, cylindrical emergency position marker whizzed through the air, hit river just yards from the patrol boat and exploded in a burst of orange smoke. Thick orange smoke. Dense enough to be seen by rescue craft a mile away. On an *open* sea, that was.

But the Rio Verde flowed through a green tunnel of jungle. Branches and vines crisscrossed above it to form an arching roof. Trapped, the smoke spread across the river like a noxious cloud. Even before Cari launched the second capsule, a thick orange haze had completely enveloped the patrol boat.

''That'll have their eyes watering,'' Dave said with grim satisfaction. ''Take us over closer to the bank and I'll...''

The pilot broke off. Reaching up to adjust his goggles, he strained against his shoulder harness.

''What?'' Cari demanded. ''What do you see?''

''Movement along the riverbank.''

''Is it Mac?''

''Hang on. I can't... Oh, crap!''

''What?'' she demanded again, her whole body twisted into a mass of tension.

''It's Mac,'' Dave confirmed tersely. ''And he's got what looks like half the patrol boat's crew on his ass.''

Cari jerked on the wheel, brought *Pegasus* around, aimed for the bank. She caught a flash of gunfire, saw the ferns part as Mac dived through them. He cut the water cleanly and went under. She didn't wait for him to surface before launching her last smoker. It went into the bank and exploded in a blossom of bright orange.

''Obstacle ahead!''

Dave's warning came at exactly the same moment the sonar gave off a loud, warning buzz. Cursing under her breath, Cari jerked the wheel again and narrowly avoided a collision with a half-sunken tree trunk. She was forced to angle away from the obstacle and wait while Mac fought the current with a strong, slicing stroke.

She felt a presence at her shoulder, knew Captain Westfall had crowded into the cockpit.

"The smoke's thinning," Dave advised grimly, his hand hovering over the missile system activation. "Do you want me to arm and lock?"

As captain of the vessel, Cari had the conn, the stick, the overall responsibility for the operation. She'd followed the rules of engagement to this point, had avoided inflicting casualties on either the government forces or the rebels. If the patrol boat started shooting, however, she'd damn well shoot back.

"Arm and lock," she ordered crisply. "Don't fire until I give the word."

Behind her, Westfall was silent. Cari gave no thought to the fact that he outranked her, that a bungled operation could mean the end of his career as well as her own. Another swift check of the instruments confirmed *Pegasus* rode high enough in the water to open the side hatch without flooding the rear compartment.

"Stand by!" she instructed those in the back via the intercom. "I'm opening the hatch."

"It's up," Kate confirmed at moment later. "I'm ready with the Survivor Retrieval System."

"Deploy SRS," Cari instructed tersely.

The SRS could shoot a lifesaving line across a mile of open sea. In this case, though, a mile of tough nylon rope presented almost as much of a problem as a solution. Kate could overshoot, tangle the rope in the trees, force them to hack free again.

She should have known Kate could handle it. All those years aboard the National Oceanic and Atmospheric Administration's hurricane hunter aircraft had taught her a thing or two about retrieval systems. She aimed for a skinny patch of sky and sent the weighted lead in a high, smooth arc. It shot up, came down again, and landed just a few feet behind Mac. The coils of lightweight rope trailing after the lead plopped down into the water all around him.

He cut his stroke, snatched at the rope, and gave a thumbs-up. Before they could reel him in, little waterspouts began to rise all around him. Cari whipped her glance to the bank, saw a figure in ragged BDUs with an automatic rifle to his shoulder stagger out of the orange pall.

"Mac's taking fire." Jill Bradshaw's voice came over the intercom, cold and deadly. "I'm in position to return it."

"Go!"

Jill let loose with a short, vicious barrage. A military cop and an expert marksman, she sent the scruffy rebel scrambling back into the orange cloud. But not before he got off a final burst.

Cari saw Mac jerk, rise out of the water a few inches, sink back under the surface.

No!

The silent scream ripped through her. Dying inside, she waited one heartbeat. Two.

Mac didn't reappear. But the nylon rope he'd been grasping did. The line curled on the river's surface, writhing like a thin, tensile snake. She keyed her mike, had opened her mouth to order Dave to take the throttles, when someone dived through the open hatch.

Sam Westfall, she saw when he broke surface and began cutting toward the spot where Mac had disappeared. The navy officer went under, came back up after long, heart-shattering moments dragging a limp form. Hooking an elbow under Mac's chin, he swam him back to *Pegasus*.

To Cari's horror, Westfall's boots churned up a sickening wake. Mac's blood was tinting the Verde from green to red. Praying as she'd never prayed before, she gripped the wheel so hard her short, trimmed nails splintered on the hard composite.

"They're aboard!" Kate relayed mere seconds later. "Get us out of here."

Slamming a fist down to close the hatch, Cari whipped the wheel around with one hand and shoved the throttle forward with the other. *Pegasus* leaped forward.

Doc Richardson was back there, she reminded herself fiercely as she steered her craft downriver. He'd stop the bleeding. Keep Mac alive. He would. He *would!*

She repeated the mantra over and over, aching to go to Mac, chained to her seat by her responsibilities as commander. Only after she'd rounded the last bend and spotted a patch of blue did she prepare to pass the baton.

"Open sky ahead, Dave."

The pilot nodded. "I'm ready. As soon as we clear these trees, I'll take us airborne."

Chapter 8

The next twenty minutes would remain forever seared in Cari's mind.

When she turned the controls over to Dave and ducked back into the rear compartment, she found Mac lying facedown on the deck in a pool of bright red blood. Cody Richardson was bent over him. He'd started an IV and had cut away Mac's shirt to expose the bullet hole in his right shoulder. Kate held the IV pack aloft, while a drenched Captain Westfall steadied himself with a hand against the bulkhead and watched every move through narrowed, steel-gray eyes.

Jill knelt on Mac's other side. As a cop, she'd seen

her share of gunshot wounds. She'd also received training in emergency medical procedures for first responders. The grim cast to her face told Cari this particular gunshot wound was bad. Very bad.

Captain Westfall confirmed that when Cari moved to his side. "Doc Richardson thinks the bullet nicked Mac's subclavian artery," he told her. "It's the main artery from the heart to the upper extremities. Doc's got to repair it fast, before Mac bleeds out."

A hard, bruising knot formed in Cari's throat. She couldn't swallow, couldn't breathe as Cody ripped open a small kit containing surgical instruments wrapped in sterile plastic. The doc was just reaching out a hand covered in a blood-drenched rubber glove when the deck shuddered under them and the kit danced out of his reach.

Swiftly, Cari retrieved it and went down on one knee beside him. "Dave's switching us to airborne mode. The next few minutes could get bumpy. Can you wait until he has us in the air?"

"No."

The terse reply stabbed into her with the vicious thrust of a bayonet. Cody didn't so much as spare her a glance.

"Every second counts right now. Get back in the cockpit and hold us as steady as you can."

Spurred by the order and a slicing fear that cut right through her, Cari sprang to her feet. She dropped into her seat and cut Dave off just as he was about to tilt the engines upward.

"Delay that. We're holding in this position until Doc gives us the green light. He's…" She forced herself to speak around that aching knot in her throat. "He's got to repair one of Mac's arteries or he might bleed to death."

"Hell!"

Dave's strong, tanned face set into rock-hard lines. He'd come late to the Pegasus cadre, brought in on short notice after the original air force representative had suffered a heart attack. As a result, he'd been forced to muscle his way inside the tight clique the other officers had already formed. In the process, he'd also bowled the vivacious Kate Hargrave right off her feet. He was part of the team now—heart and soul. The possibility they might lose one of their own hit him almost as hard as it did Cari.

He recovered swiftly. He had no choice. He'd faced that grim possibility before, as had every other member of the Pegasus cadre. It came with wearing the uniform of their country.

Mouth tight, Cari eyed the swirling currents ahead. They were drifting fast toward the point where the river emptied into the lagoon. To keep the craft steady, they'd have to fight both the drag of the sea and the force of the waves rolling in from the outer reef. The maneuver would require every bit of Cari's seamanship and then some. Setting her jaw, she forced herself to concentrate on the task at hand.

"I'll take the controls. You keep an eye on the radar screen. If those bastards in the patrol boat come within range," she promised savagely, "they're gonna suck in something other than orange smoke this time."

Cari forgot all about the patrol boat when Captain Westfall came forward long, agonizing moments later.

"Doc's stopped the hemorrhaging."

She slumped back against her seat. Closing her eyes, she sent a silent prayer of thanks winging upward. Westfall's next words brought her jerking upright again.

"Mac's not out of the woods yet. He's lost a lot of blood and the bullet did some serious damage to tissue and bone. We need to get him to a first-class medical facility, fast."

That let out the forward operating base in Nicaragua, Cari realized with a sick feeling in her stomach. Their medical facility consisted of two tents.

"We'll have to head back to Corpus," she said tightly.

"Have you got enough fuel to take us in?"

"No," Dave answered after a quick check of the

gauges, "but we can request a tanker to pass us some gas enroute."

"Do it."

The terse command underscored the continuing urgency of the situation. Cari didn't need a second order.

"Tell everyone in the back to buckle up," she bit out, then tacked on a belated, "sir."

Since Dave had piloted *Pegasus* on its first flight, she acted as copilot while he raced through the procedures to compete the transition from sea to air mode. Mere minutes later, he tilted the engines upright. Moments more, and *Pegasus* lifted straight up into a hover. The steamy green of the jungle was below, an endless marriage of turquoise sea and azure sky ahead. Then Dave brought the craft's nose down, angled the engines again and applied full power. Caribe fell away behind them.

Cari got on the mike before they'd cleared the reef ringing the island. The USAF Coordination Center agreed to scramble a KC-135 out of Barksdale AFB, Louisiana. The tanker would hook up with them over the Gulf and supply both *Pegasus* and the Pavehawk helicopter with fuel, which indicated it would tail them back to Corpus Christi.

Her next hook-up was to the Operations Center at

the Corpus Christi Naval Air Station. The controller promised to have an ambulance waiting when *Pegasus* touched down.

With its faster speed, *Pegasus* beat the Pavehawk back to Corpus by several hours.

The promised ambulance was waiting to whisk Doc and Mac to the Naval Hospital. With the wail of the siren knifing into her heart, Cari helped Dave shut down *Pegasus*. Once the multimillion-dollar vehicle was secure, Captain Westfall disappeared into the Mobile Control Center to make a report of the mission to his superiors via secure comm. Cari didn't stick around to provide additional input. She and Dave and the rest of the team raced to the hospital.

Mac had already been wheeled into the operating room. He was still there when the Whites and their charges arrived at the surgical waiting room where the Pegasus crew was camped out. The missionaries looked harried, the children a little frightened, and the U.S. Customs Agent accompanying them distinctly disapproving.

While Dave, Jill and Kate helped settle the kids in front of the TV with soft drinks and candy bars from a nearby vending machine, the customs agent confronted Cari.

''I understand you made the decision to bring these children out of Caribe.''

''That's correct.''

"I also understand they have no papers or emigration documents of any sort."

"We left Caribe in something of a hurry," she replied with considerable understatement.

The agent pursed his lips. He was a short, pudgy man with damp stains ringing the armpits of his white uniform shirt and a plastic nameplate that gave his name as Scroggins.

"I'll have to notify the Immigration and Naturalization Service," he said with a shake of his head. "INS is responsible for minors arriving in the States unaccompanied by relatives or legal guardians."

"I've told you," Janice White snapped. "Reverend White and I are their ex officio guardians. At least until we can contact the families who've agreed to take them in."

"But you have no papers granting you that authority."

"We have copies of our applications," Harry White put in earnestly. "To the Caribe authorities, the U.S. government, and our church sponsors."

"Applications aren't good enough. Sorry, folks. My hands are tied. I have to notify the INS. They'll take the kids into administrative custody and hold them until their status is resolved."

Cari's lips curled back. She leaned forward, got two inches from the man's nose. "The hell they will!"

Startled, Scroggins took an involuntary step back. "Hey, Lieutenant, I'm just doing my job."

She'd seen this coming, had witnessed too many heartbroken refugees being taken into custody for deportation back to the very country they'd risked their lives to escape. She'd also had a good idea of the bureaucratic battle the Whites would face once they landed in the States. But that was before Mac had taken a bullet trying to get these kids to safety. Before Doc had worked feverishly to keep the marine from bleeding to death. Before the aching fear that he wouldn't make it had carved a permanent hole in Cari's gut.

Captain Westfall must have sensed she was about to tell the customs rep what he could do with his job. He cut in smoothly, wielding his authority like a blade.

"We appreciate that you have certain responsibilities, Agent Scroggins. For your information, I concurred with Lieutenant Dunn's decision to transport these children out of Caribe. Please inform the INS representative to contact me personally on this matter."

The customs official wilted under the captain's cool stare. "Yes, sir. I'll do that."

Cari bit her lip. Westfall *had* concurred with her decision—but only after the fact. And after some rather choice words on the subject of sidestepping in-

ternational law. She didn't want him to take the heat
for her actions, but training and respect for rank went
bone deep. Junior officers didn't contradict their superiors in public. Particularly when said superior sent
her a look that suggested she'd be smart at this point
to keep her mouth shut.

"Thanks," Janice White said when Scroggins had
scurried off to make his call to the INS. Shagging a
hand through her short, blond crop, she gave the captain a thorough once-over. They'd met only briefly
during the transfer from *Pegasus* to the Pavehawk.
Evidently the captain passed inspection.

"Harry and I better get busy and make some calls.
Hopefully, we can reach each of the families who've
applied to adopt the children before the INS shows
up."

"Why don't I line you up with some temporary
quarters here on base?" Westfall suggested. "You
can get the kids fed and cleaned up, then make your
calls."

"Fed and cleaned up would be wonderful."

"Give me a list of what you need for them in the
way of clothes, food and games or books. I'll see it's
taken care of."

"It could be a long list."

The captain gave her one of his rare, flinty smiles.
"I can handle it."

She tipped her head and measured him with those cool green eyes. "Yes, I imagine you can."

His gaze followed her as she moved to the small group clustered around the Reverend White.

"They make quite a pair."

"Yes, they do. Harry told me she gave up a very lucrative private practice to assist him in Caribe. He thinks the world of his sister."

"Sister?"

The captain's glance lasered back to Cari. Despite the weight of her worry over Mac, she formed the distinct impression that she'd snared Westfall's full attention with that bit of information.

"Sister," she confirmed. "Our intel on the Whites was a little incomplete."

"Hmm."

With that noncommittal reply, the captain walked to the wall phone and requested a connection to the naval air station C.O. He was back a few minutes later with word that the Whites and their charges could stay at the Transient Lodging Facility until they'd squared matters with the INS.

"I've got a car outside," he told the missionaries. "I'll drive you over."

The arrangements suited everyone but Paulo. For a child with no larynx, he'd developed rather expressive means of communicating. In this instance, it was by crossing his arms, pushing out his lower lip and refusing to vacate the chair he was occupying.

"It could be several hours yet," Janice White told him patiently.

The lip stayed pushed.

"Lieutenant Dunn will let us know the moment Major McIver is out of surgery," Reverend White chimed in, throwing Cari a look of silent appeal. "Won't you?"

"Yes, of course."

Obviously unconvinced, Paulo uncrossed his thin arms and signed an urgent message. Janice White interpreted.

"He says he wants to stay here. Harry, can you manage the others? I'll wait with Paulo."

"There's no need for that," Kate Hargrave countered. Smiling, she hooked a stray tendril of gleaming auburn behind her left ear. "There are enough of us here to keep an eye on him."

Janice eyed the weather scientist with a combination of relief and doubt. "Are you sure? It's difficult to understand him if you don't sign."

"One of my nephews is deaf. I'm not real fast at speaking, but I can read the basics like French fries, cheeseburgers and the latest X Box video game titles."

"All right then."

Turning to the boy, Janice issued some instructions

in Caribe. He signaled his agreement with a quick nod. Satisfied, Janice started to push to her feet. A tug on her baggy tan slacks stopped her in half crouch. Paulo looked from her to Cari and flashed a series of hand signals.

"He wants to know if you still have his knife," the missionary related.

"What? Oh, yes. I do."

It took some digging, but she found it in one of the side pockets of her BDU pants. She held it out, palm up, and the boy snatched it up.

In the midst of her misery over Mac, Cari had room for a new ache. That rusted bit of steel was the kid's most precious possession. He'd offered it to her back in Caribe to aid Mac. Now, he clutched it in a tight, grubby fist while he kept vigil with her.

Their wait lasted another agonizing forty minutes.

The INS agent came, took statements and left again to find the Whites. She was a calm, precise type who came across as considerably more sympathetic to the children's plight than Agent Scroggins had. Her wry admission that the Immigration and Naturalization Service had recently been slapped with a class-action suit on behalf of the more than eight thousand children they held in detention, most of whom couldn't speak English and had no inkling of their rights, might have had something to do with her promise to grease the skids if possible.

After that there was nothing to do but pace the hall. Cari did take one side trip to the ladies' room, only to stare blankly at the straggle-haired harridan in the mirror. Her BDUs showed the effects of a night spent stretched out on a straw mat and repeated dunkings in the Rio Verde. Her eyes looked haunted. Makeup was only a distant memory.

Impatiently, she splashed cold water on her cheeks and tugged a comb borrowed from Kate through her tangles. A quick twist and a plastic clip anchored the dark brown mass on top of her head. She was back, wearing a path in tile so bright and clean it still stank of pine-scented antiseptic, when Doc Richardson pushed through the double doors leading from the surgical unit.

He caught the instant attention of everyone in the waiting room, and the look on his face started Cari's heart pumping pure terror. She froze, unable to move, to think, to breathe, while he walked the length of the corridor.

Paulo, too, saw the physician's approach. Wiggling out of his chair, he moved to Cari's side and slid his hand into hers. They stood side by side, their fingers locked in a bone-crunching grip, until Doc sliced through their paralyzing tension.

"He's going to make it."

Cari's breath left on a long whoosh. The small hand gripping hers squeezed tighter in a reflex of silent, heartfelt relief. Cody gave the group a few moments to savor the good news before delivering the rest of his report.

"The bullet tore through Mac's muscle and pulverized his right shoulder. The surgeons here patched him up as best they could, but he's looking at eventual replacement of the entire joint."

Cari swallowed hard. "Can they do that? Replace an entire shoulder?"

"The procedure isn't as simple or as common as a hip or knee replacement, but it's doable."

Doc scraped a palm across his jaw. Like the rest of the Pegasus team, he was showing the effects of the past few days. Dark bristles shadowed his cheeks and chin. His eyes were rimmed with red.

"I'm not real up on the stats for that particular orthopedic procedure," he said quietly. "I do know patients have a fairly high chance of recovering at least partial use of their arms."

Cari was so relieved it took a moment or two for the full import of that "partial" to sink in. They were talking about all-or-nothing, you're-in-or-you're-out Russ McIver here. The man who'd found not only a profession, but a home in the United States Marine Corps.

Something perilously close to pity fluttered deep in

the pit of her stomach. She'd just begun to discover the man behind the marine. Had shared only a few shattering kisses. Yet she knew with gut-wrenching certainty Mac wouldn't settle for "partial" use of anything. He'd go for one hundred percent no matter how long it took or how much pain he endured in the process.

"Is he conscious?" she asked Doc. "Can we see him?"

"They're moving him out of Recovery into a room as we speak. I'll take you to him."

Chapter 9

The room was typical of military hospitals. Walls painted in what was probably meant as a soothing cream and tan color scheme. Two beds, only one of them occupied. Floors so clean Cari's boot-soles squeaked when she entered.

Paulo still gripped her hand. The boy's face settled into its habitual scowl as he viewed the figure stretched out in the bed. Mac lay propped over toward his good side, with mounds of pillows at his back. The bandages swathing his injured shoulder showed snowy-white against his tan.

Doc Richardson ran an assessing eye over the patient before dragging him from his drugged stupor.

"Wake up, McIver. You've got people here who want to say hello."

Mac's right eyebrow inched up. Slowly, one lid lifted. The dilated pupil indicated anesthetic was still swimming through his veins, but he seemed to recognize at least one face in the crowd.

"Ca…ri."

She loosened her death grip on the boy's fingers. Dropping into the chair beside the bed, she snaked a wrist through the bed rails and found Mac's good hand. A smile trembled on her lips.

"You gave us a helluva scare, big guy."

"Did…I?" He blinked a few times, obviously struggling to focus. "What…happened?"

"You took a bullet in your right shoulder."

He scrunched his forehead. "The…kids?"

"They're okay. The Pavehawk brought them into Corpus a few hours behind us. In fact…"

Without letting go of Mac, she hooked her elbow in the air and motioned for Paulo to duck under it. He came up inside the circle of her arm, mere inches from Mac's face. Somehow the wounded marine summoned enough strength to arrange his still-slack features into a lopsided grin.

"Hey, pal. You…made…it."

Paulo responded with a series of quick, flashing hand signals, which Kate took a stab at interpreting. "He says we should have taken him with us when we went back for you. He wouldn't have let you get shot.''

"Next…time, kid.''

The haze in Mac's eyes was slowly dissipating. Pain slipped in to take its place. Cari noted the crease that formed between his brows, the pinched look at the corners of his mouth. Doc Richardson picked up on the same signs.

"Feeling that shoulder, are you?''

Mac responded with a grunt.

"I'll get the nurse to administer your pain medication.''

Doc made for the exit just as Captain Westfall returned from seeing the Whites and the other children settled in temporary quarters. The captain's BDUs showed the aftereffects of his dive into the Rio Verde and dark bristles shadowed his cheeks and chin. Yet when he entered, he carried with him the charged atmosphere and aura of command Cari had come to associate with the man. The usual flint was gone from his eyes when he stood beside Mac's bed, though.

"Good to see you awake, McIver.''

"Good to…*be* awake, sir.''

"You and Lieutenant Dunn did one fine job getting the Whites and those kids out of Caribe.''

"Let's hope the INS agrees,'' Cari muttered.

"Prob…lem?''

She lifted her shoulders. "Pretty much the bureaucratic B.S. we expected. Nothing we can't handle."

She could tell from his expression he didn't quite buy the breezy explanation but was too weak to demand details. What he needed at this point, Cody Richardson suggested when the nurse arrived with his pain medication, was rest. Lots of it.

Cari hated leaving Mac like this, weak and hurting. Fact of the matter was, she hated leaving him at all.

"He'll be okay."

At Cody's quiet assurance, Cari untangled her fingers from Mac's grip and eased her hand between the bed-rail bars. "I'll come back later," she told him. "After I've washed off the stink from the Rio Verde."

He managed a nod that led to a wince, followed by a fierce scowl reminiscent of Paulo at his most belligerent. Cari didn't envy the nurse waiting to dope him up. Something told her Mac wasn't going to make the best patient. She started to push out of the chair, was startled when he brought his good arm over the rail and snagged the lapels of her shirt.

"Good…job, Dunn."

"Back at you, McIver."

Pain carved a deep furrow between his brows, but he flexed his bicep and tugged her down.

"Mac, what…?"

That's all she got out before he dragged her down

the last inch or so and covered her mouth with his. The kiss didn't compare to his previous efforts in either skill or duration, but it was enough to stop Cari's breath in her throat.

"La...ter," Mac muttered, releasing her shirt.

"Later," she agreed softly.

Levering upward, she turned to face a solid wall of spectators. Kate wore a gleeful expression. Jill looked smug. Cody and Dave were grinning. Captain Westfall maintained a noncommittal air, but Cari noted he didn't look at all surprised by the fact that two of his subordinates seemed to have developed a close sense of teamwork on this mission. A *very* close sense of teamwork.

Cari knew she was in for a grilling later, after they'd finished the post-mission debrief. Hopefully she'd have an answer ready by then that would satisfy the lively curiosity dancing in her friends' eyes.

Thankfully, Kate and Jill waited until the team had cleaned up and finished the grueling four-hour debrief to demand an explanation. The two women rapped on the door to Cari's room in the naval air station's visiting officers' quarters just as she was getting ready to head back to the hospital. After months of sharing a cramped modular unit in New Mexico, all three were enjoying the privacy and space afforded by their separate quarters. Privacy only went so far, though, as Kate proved when she aimed a finger square at Cari's chest and marched her back into the sitting room.

"Okay, girl. We want details."

Like Cari, Kate had changed out of her uniform. The weather officer's jeans and fuzzy red knit tank top clung to her lush curves. Jill, too, wore jeans. Hers were paired with a crisp white blouse and black leather belt that cinched her slim waist. Mirroring Kate's avid curiosity, the cop plopped down in the sitting room's only comfortable chair.

"What the heck happened down there in the jungle between you and Mac?"

"We took *Pegasus* in," Cari replied with deliberately provocative brevity. "Brought the Whites and the kids out. Ironed out a few of our, ah, differences."

Kate gave a huff of derision. "Nice try, Dunn. Back up and expand on the ironing part."

Shoving her hands in the front pockets of her jeans, Cari hunched her shoulders. "I thought it was just the adrenaline," she admitted. "The first time Mac kissed me, we were both strung tight as anchor cables."

"The *first* time," Kate echoed. Waggling her brows, she shot Jill a knowing look. "Ha! I told you."

"Okay, okay." The blonde threw up her hands in good-natured defeat. "You win."

"I bet her a dinner of char-grilled red snapper that

hospital smooch wasn't the first time you'd locked lips with our resident leatherneck," Kate explained with smug satisfaction.

"Jill should have known better than to bet with you," Cari said, laughing.

Kate possessed unerring instincts, a nose for fine nuances and an intelligence network that rivaled the CIA's. She'd picked up on Jill's attraction to Cody long before the rest of the team had a clue about it. The scientist had also ignited a blaze of her own with tall, tanned Dave Scott, but she made it clear she hadn't come to talk about anyone but Cari and Mac.

"The first time you kissed you were both strung tight," she prompted, hitching a hip on the arm of the sofa. "And the second time?"

"I was strung pretty tight then, too," Cari confessed. "So tight I came close to forgetting that I was under orders and on a mission."

Kate sobered instantly. Fooling around was one thing. Fooling around to the point where it jeopardized a crew or an operation was an entirely different matter.

"But you didn't forget."

"No, I didn't. It was touch and go there for a while, though."

Looking back, Cari couldn't believe how ferociously she'd ached to drag Mac down to the spongy earth. Even now her nipples tightened at the memory of his hands and teeth and tongue working their magic on her body.

"What about Jerry?"

Jill's question sliced through the haze of sensual memories. Wrenched back to the present, Cari grimaced.

"I ended things with Jerry before I left for Caribe. By e-mail, I'm embarrassed to admit."

"Why are you embarrassed? Didn't he propose electronically?"

"Yes, but…"

"Hey, it wasn't like you had time for anything else," Kate pointed out. Curiosity brimmed in her green eyes. "How did Commander Wharton take his marching orders?"

"I don't know. I haven't checked my e-mail since I got back."

She didn't intend to, either, until she got back from the hospital. There wasn't room in her head for anyone else but Mac right now.

Kate was like a dog with a juicy bone. She wouldn't let go. "Okay, so you dumped Jerry and almost got it on with Mac. Where do you and our macho marine go from here?"

Cari had already asked herself that question. Several times. She still hadn't come up with an answer. Snagging her purse, she hooked the strap over her shoulder.

"*I'm* going back to the hospital."

Her two friends scrambled to their feet. "We'll go with you."

The entire test cadre popped into Mac's room at various times that evening, but the pain medication had knocked him out. He slept through their visits and straight through the night, the charge nurse reported to Cari the next afternoon. She also confirmed Cari's suspicion that Mac would make a less than optimal patient.

"He insisted on going to the head under his own steam this morning," the navy nurse drawled. "Would have fallen flat on his face if we hadn't rushed in and caught him."

Her glance went to her patient, now attempting one-handed spins in his wheelchair. He was surrounded by the giggling swarm of youngsters who'd come to visit him.

"Typical marine," the nurse murmured with a mixture of exasperation, affection and admiration. "I expect we'll have to tie him down to get him to rest."

"I expect you will."

She moved off, and Cari joined Janice White at the edge of the small crowd surrounding Mac.

"Good morning, Doc."

"'Morning, Caroline." Smiling, she took in Cari's freshly shampooed hair, dusting of makeup and sharply pressed khakis. "I see you washed away the Rio Verde."

"So did you."

The missionary had shed her jungle grunginess and taken on a whole new aura. In a slim black skirt, strappy sandals and sleeveless pink top that brought out the strawberry highlights in her blond hair, she looked cool and competent and years younger than Cari had thought her.

The kids had undergone the same transformation, she saw. Gone were the ragged shorts and hand-me-down shirts. Rosa beamed amid the ruffles and frills of a Barbie-doll blue dress. Little Tomas couldn't see his spiffy high-top sneakers but obviously delighted in the tinkling tune they emitted. He stood with legs widespread, lifting first one foot, then the other, and added a musical beat to the proceedings. Paulo, Cari saw with a smile, sported a brand-new Spider-Man T-shirt. This one was done in Day-Glo colors that lit up the hospital corridor in electric red and blue.

"When did you find time to take the kids shopping?"

"Sam came by last night and hauled us all to the local mall."

Sam, was it? Cari swallowed a grin. Captain Westfall certainly hadn't wasted any time making good on his offer of aid and assistance.

Her inclination to smile fled as little Rosa clambered into Mac's lap, however. The girl's malformed spine made the maneuver difficult and she accidentally knocked against the arm strapped tight against Mac's chest. His jaw went rigid, but he waved Janice back when she would have retrieved the girl.

"She's okay."

He relaxed enough to give Cari a crooked grin. "Hi, Lieutenant."

"Hi yourself."

"Want a ride after I wheel Rosa down the corridor a few times?"

"I'll think about it."

"Don't trust my driving, huh? And here I trusted you to steer me across an open ocean."

"*Pegasus* comes better equipped. With navigational aids," she added hastily when he sent her a wicked look.

Beside her, Janice White choked back a laugh. The two women watched him sail down the corridor with Rosa planted firmly in his lap.

"How are you doing with INS?" Cari asked over Rosa's high-pitched squeals.

"Harry's still battling with them. We spent an hour on the phone last night contacting the families who've applied to adopt the children. We explained that they'll have to stand as sponsors to the children until the INS works out their legal status. Most of the couples are flying into Corpus Christi today."

Cari shot her a quick look. "Most of them?"

The missionary blew out a breath. "Turns out the folks who applied to adopt Paulo are in the middle of rather nasty divorce proceedings."

"Oh, no!"

"Unfortunately, they didn't bother to notify our church adoption agency that their marriage had fallen apart. The agency is scrambling now to find another home for Paulo. It might take a while, though, given the expensive surgery he's facing."

Cari's glance went back to the boy. The Whites must have told him the news. He stood a little apart from the others, observing but not participating. The sparkle had gone out of his brown eyes and his face was once again a sullen mask.

"INS is insisting they have to take him into protective custody pending deportation," Janice said quietly. "He's not particularly happy about the prospect."

Neither was Mac, Cari discovered when he wheeled back down the corridor with Rosa still perched in his lap. Tomas followed the squeak of the chair, his sneakers beeping out a merry rhythm. The other kids tagged along, as well. All except Paulo, who maintained his distance.

Mac's gaze lingered on the boy for a moment before meeting Cari's. "Janice tell you about Paulo?"

''Yes. What a bummer.''

''Did she also tell you about the INS detention centers?''

''They're supposed to be administrative holding centers,'' the missionary said when Cari shook her head. ''The kids put into these centers don't know that, though. Most of them think they're being punished. They don't speak English, don't understand their rights and, unlike adults detained by the INS, aren't eligible for release after posting bond. They spend weeks or months until deportation in bare cells, sometimes with local youths accused of violent crimes.''

The thought of Paulo locked in with young toughs spawned a sick feeling in Cari's stomach. The boy had endured so much in his own country. Now, just when he thought he'd found a safe haven in the United States, he'd be thrown to the sharks again.

''The Berks County Youth Center in Pennsylvania serves as the INS detention center for the East Coast,'' Janice continued, her voice grim. ''They had the kids doing push-ups for every infraction of the rules. It took a class-action suit to make them admit most of the children couldn't *understand* these so-called rules.''

Mac's jaw set. His eyes went flat for a moment, as though he was seeing things he'd rather forget.

"It's not going to happen," he said flatly. "I want to talk to this INS official."

"She wants to talk to you, too," Cari told him. "She took statements from the rest of us yesterday afternoon and said she'd come by for yours today."

"Fine. I'll have a thing or two to say to her."

Cari didn't doubt it, but she knew as well as Mac that talking wouldn't hack it with the INS. She was turning over possible options in her mind when the charge nurse swooped down on the small group.

"Your surgeon will be making rounds soon, Major. I refuse to let him find you in the hall doing wheelies. You need to be in bed."

"We'll leave," Janice said, lifting Rosa into her arms. "The kids just wanted to see for their own eyes that Major Mac was all right."

Cari stayed her with a quick request. "Can you hang loose a few minutes?"

"Sure."

"I'll be right back. I just need to make a phone call."

She was back some moments later and relayed the gist of her conversation to Janice, who hustled the kids out of the ward so she could in turn relay the news to her brother.

Cari waited until the nurse and an aide had Mac settled before entering his room. He was stretched out on the smoothed white sheets, his face turned to the dazzling October sunlight streaming in through wide windows. They gave a sweeping view of the naval base and the aquamarine waters of the Gulf of Mexico beyond.

She guessed from Mac's fierce frown that he wasn't concentrating on the view. He confirmed as much when he turned at the sound of her footsteps on the tiled floor.

''Paulo's not going into a detention center, Cari. Not if I can help it. I know the kind of scars they can leave on a boy like him.''

The kind that faded, but never quite went away, she guessed.

Mac had never talked about himself in the months they'd spent together in New Mexico, had never mentioned his family that she could recall. Cari had picked up only bits and pieces of his background.

As chief of security for the Pegasus project, Jill Bradshaw had access to the complete security dossiers on all assigned personnel. Jill took her responsibilities too seriously to ever divulge details from those dossiers. Kate, on the other hand, had experienced no qualms about activating her informal intelligence network to come up with tidbits of essential information. Like the fact that Mac had joined the marines before finishing high school. That he'd never married. That he'd been wounded twice, once in Afghanistan, once in the Iraqi War.

This was Cari's first hint that he'd been wounded well before he joined the corps. She wanted to probe, to learn more about the man who'd bulldozed his way into her heart, but the closed, tight expression on Mac's face didn't invite questions. Saving them for later, she perched on the edge of his bed.

"I think I might have won Paulo a reprieve."

"How?"

"I called my sister, Deborah. She and her husband are currently raising two dogs, two cats and four kids, with another about to make an appearance. Their house has all the calm of Grand Central Station during peak rush hour, but Deb insists there's room for Paulo until the Whites' church locates another family for him."

The grim expression on Mac's face eased into one of relief tinged with only a shade of doubt. "Sounds like the perfect place for the kid. Think he'll be able to make himself understood in that crowd?"

Cari laughed. "Paulo doesn't seem to have much difficulty making himself understood in *any* crowd. Deb said she and Jack will drive down from Shreveport as soon as he can get someone to fill in for him at work. We'll have to hold off INS until they get here."

Mac's eyes glinted. "I think we can manage that. In the meantime…"

"Yes?"

He reached up with his good hand, snagged the lapel of her khaki uniform shirt. "I have this hazy recollection of talking to you last night. And a promise of later."

"Remember that, do you?"

"Oh, yeah."

Bracing her hands on either side of the bed to make sure she didn't jar his injured shoulder, she leaned over him.

Chapter 10

Cari spent the next few days in a whirl of worry and frenetic activity.

The Pegasus team holed up in their mobile command center to evaluate their craft's performance in actual operations and prepare a detailed report for the Joint Chiefs of Staff. Captain Westfall was scheduled to deliver the report in person the following week.

Mac drafted his input in his hospital room and gradually began to make brief forays to join the rest of the team at the command center. He regained strength daily, if not the use of his right arm. Fretting at his impaired movement, he was forced to await an evaluation from orthopedic surgeons as to when they could replace his shattered shoulder joint before being discharged from the hospital.

"It's more a question of *if* they can replace the joint, not *when*," Doc Richardson confided to Cari after escorting the increasingly restless patient back to the hospital. "The procedure requires sufficient bone to anchor the replacement joint. Given the damage that bullet did to Mac's shoulder, he may not be a candidate for the surgery."

Side by side, they walked out of the hospital into the bright October sunlight. The stiff breeze blowing in off the Gulf carried a salty tang, but Cari paid no attention to the scent that usually stirred her senses.

"Will he regain use of his arm without the surgery?"

"Some use, certainly."

For anyone else, "some" might be enough. But not for her all-or-nothing, one hundred percent, gung ho marine. Concern over how Mac would adjust to a future that might include limited capabilities to perform his duties nibbled away at the edges of Cari's overwhelming relief that he'd beat the odds and survived the bullet.

She knew the choices that lay ahead of him. If surgery to reconstruct his shoulder wasn't an option, Mac would go before a military medical evaluation board to determine his suitability for continued service. The eval board could decide to retain him on restricted duty or recommend him for a disability retirement.

A tight knot formed smack in the middle of her chest at the thought. The Pegasus team had already lost one of their own to medical retirement. Lieutenant Colonel Bill Thompson, the original air force rep to the cadre, had suffered a heart attack after contracting the virus that had swept through the isolated site. As a result, he'd been yanked off the team and replaced by Dave Scott.

"How long before Mac learns whether he's a candidate for the surgery?" she asked Cody.

"The surgeons here sent his X rays and records to two of the country's top orthopedic surgeons who specialize in shoulder replacements. Hopefully, we'll hear something back within a few days."

In the midst of Cari's worries over Mac and her work on the report detailing *Pegasus*'s seaworthiness, officials from the adoption agency run by the Whites' church flew in to iron matters out with the INS. They also expedited legal proceedings and helped with the first meetings between the children and their prospective parents. The couples themselves flew in from all parts of the country, some nervous, all excited. One by one, the children departed with their new families. The departures were a wrenching mixture of joy and wariness as the kids exchanged the familiar if bleak past for an unknown future.

Paulo remained with the Whites, who delayed their departure from Corpus until his situation was resolved. Faced with the combined resistance of the missionaries, the Pegasus team and one very determined marine, INS held off taking the boy into custody pending evaluation of Cari's sister and brother-in-law as temporary guardians.

Deborah and Jack drove down from Shreveport late Friday afternoon. They arrived with all four kids and, thankfully, only one household pet in tow. Trading her uniform for a pair of floppy sandals, comfortable slacks and a red-checkered blouse, Cari met them at the beachside condo on Padre Island she'd rented for them. It sat near the northern tip of the island, close enough to watch the fishing fleet putting out from Aransas Pass but far enough away from the docks to avoid the fish aroma that permeated the air when the fleet returned.

When the Hamilton family piled out of their SUV, laughter bubbled up in Cari's throat at the chaos that ensued. Her two nieces and two nephews whooped with delight at being released from their seat belts and car seats. They treated their aunt to bear hugs and wet, sloppy kisses before making a beeline for the sandy beach. The chocolate-colored, full-sized poodle Deb had tried to pawn off on every one of her relatives lumbered alongside the kids, emitting earsplitting woofs of joy.

"No going in the water without one of us there to supervise!" their father shouted. The kids swerved in time to avoid the surf. Pierre the Poodle plowed right in.

Undaunted by the prospect of coping with a wet animal the size of a small horse, Deb levered her very pregnant self out of the car and enveloped her sister in a fierce hug. She and Cari were about the same height, with the cinnamon dark eyes and glossy mink-brown hair that ran in their family, but the similarities ended there. Deb dabbled in watercolors, loved any and all sweets and had married her first and only love right out of high school. She took vicarious delight in her sister's adventures in uniform, but shuddered at the thought of being subjected to anything resembling military discipline herself.

Cari returned her hug and that of her big, ham-fisted brother-in-law. It had always amazed her how perfectly her petite sister and this high-school-football-star-turned-math-teacher fit together.

"Thanks for coming to the rescue like this. I owe you, Jack."

"Don't think I won't collect, too." His blue eyes laughed down at her. "Deb and I plan to dump kids, dogs, cats, parakeets and gerbils on Aunt Cari one of these days and take off for a blissful week of solitude.''

"Any time. Just give me a little advance notice.''

"Advance *warning,* you mean. You'll need at least twenty-four hours to batten down the hatches and do whatever else you coast guard types do before a hurricane hits.'' Waving aside her offer of assistance, he shooed the two women toward the condo. "You girls go on inside. I'll bring the bags and the rest of the tribe.''

Hooking her arm in her sister's, Cari escorted her to the beachside cottage. It was an airy, four-bedroom unit with additional sleep sofas in the living room, a fully equipped kitchen and a breathtaking view of the Gulf. It was also, Cari had been assured by the rental agent, kid- and dog-proof. Evidently this particular condo catered to families on vacation as well as the sun-seeking and often rowdy college-age hoards that descended on Padre Island every spring break.

"Oh, man,'' Deb breathed when she viewed the dunes rolling right to the sliding glass doors. "The kids are going to love this place. They'll also bury this carpet in about six inches of sand.''

"Not to worry. I suspect that's why the rental agency put in sisal carpets. It's tough enough to withstand sand and wet feet. I stocked the fridge for you. Want some Triple Fudge Ripple?''

"You sweetheart!'' Keeping one eye on her kids

through the sliding glass doors, she sank into one of the chairs grouped around a glass-topped table. "Pile a bowl full for both of us and tell me more about Paulo."

"We don't know much about his background," Cari said as she heaped ice cream into two bowls. "Janice White—one of the missionaries who brought him out of Caribe—says he just showed up at their mission a year or so ago, half starved and sporting a set of vicious bruises. From what they can gather, the rebels killed his mother. There's no record of his father. There's no record of Paulo, either, which adds to the complications of his, uh, precipitous departure from Caribe."

"A departure you had something to do with, I take it."

"Right. I can't go into details, just that Mac and I were sent in to extract the Whites. The kids came with them."

"Who's Mac?"

"A marine I've been working with for the past few months."

She didn't use any particular inflection, but Deb's spoon paused halfway between bowl and mouth.

"A few months, huh?"

"We've been assigned to a special project."

"Is he cute?"

"Cute, no. Rugged and compelling, most definitely."

"I see." Catlike, Deb swiped her tongue along the back of her spoon. "Just out of curiosity, where does your lawyer friend fit into this equation?"

"He doesn't," Cari admitted. "I broke things off with Jerry."

"Thank goodness!"

Startled by her sister's emphatic response, Cari blinked.

"None of us in the family thought he was right for you," her sister confided. "We also thought you were crazy to give up a career you love to become a stay-at-home mom."

"That's interesting, coming from a woman who takes such joy in doing just that."

"Isn't it?" Complacently, Deb downed another spoonful of ice cream. "But then I never wanted anything else. You, on the other hand, decided to join the coast guard almost the first week the family moved to Maryland."

That was true. After investing in a home on a spit of the Chesapeake's eastern shore, their parents had purchased a sailboat. Before they'd let any of their lively brood set so much as a toe aboard the sleek twenty-four-footer, however, they'd enrolled them in a water-safety course conducted by the local coast guard auxiliary. The tanned, curly-haired sailor who'd conducted the course had fascinated the thirteen-year-old Cari. The bits and pieces she'd learned about the coast guard's mission had come to fascinate her even more. She'd applied to the U.S. Coast Guard Academy, had been accepted right out of college, and never looked back.

Until the urge to nest had started to ping at her, that is. Now she wanted it all. Her career. A family. Mac.

Almost the instant the thought formed, Cari rejected it. Sometime in the past few weeks, her priorities had inexorably altered. The order of importance was now Mac first, a family and her career second.

The realization hit her with gale force impact. She wanted Mac. Period. In any way, shape or form she could get him. Everything else would have to fall in after him.

Now, she thought wryly, all she had to do was determine what Mac's priorities were.

She got her first inkling later that afternoon, when she escorted her sister to her first meeting with Paulo. Jack stayed with the kids, having decided it was best not to bombard the boy with their whole tribe right away. Instead, Deb brought pictures of the family and their home in Shreveport to show Paulo.

They arranged to meet the Whites and their charge

at the hospital. Harry and Janice were in the waiting room when the two sisters arrived. With the Whites was one of the counselors from their church's adoption agency.

"Paulo's down the hall with Major Mac," Janice explained. "We wanted a chance to talk with you first, Mrs. Hamilton, and answer any questions you might have about the boy."

Nodding, Deb lowered herself into one of the waiting room's armchairs. The missionaries took seats facing her, the official from their church just behind them. He was a slight, scholarly looking gentleman in neatly pressed tan Dockers, a blue oxford shirt, and a red polka-dot bow tie. Introducing himself to Cari and Deb, Henry Easton explained a little about his mission and the difficulties of placing children with disabilities such as Paulo.

"You understand he was born without a larynx."

"Cari told me. She also said an artificial voice box could be implanted."

"That's correct," Easton confirmed. "Our church had arranged to share the costs with the couple who'd applied to adopt Paulo, as their insurance wouldn't cover preexisting conditions. Now, of course, we'll have to put the operation on hold until we screen other prospective parents for the boy."

"Or our bishop convinces the doctors involved to

donate their time and skills," Harry White put in. "He's pretty good at arm-twisting."

"Which is why Harry and I will be on another plane less than a week after hotfooting it out of Caribe," Janice said dryly. "But only after we get Paulo settled. He carries some psychological scars in addition to his physical disability," she warned. "He wouldn't tell us much about what happened before he came to us, but from what we could gather he saw his mother raped and shot by the rebels."

"Dear Lord!" Pity flooded Deb's brown eyes. "What about his father?"

"He doesn't know who his father is, or was. Nor does the Caribe government." She hesitated, let her glance linger on Deb's rounded belly. "You have four children of your own and another on the way. Are you sure you want to take on one more, even temporarily?"

Cari smiled as her sister's chin lifted to a determined angle. Anyone in Deb's rambunctious family would have recognized the warning signals and immediately ceased doing whatever had generated that look.

"I'm sure," she said firmly. "So is my husband. We wouldn't have driven down from Shreveport otherwise."

Satisfied, Janice nodded and sat back. Deb wasn't quite finished yet. Turning to the church officials, she demonstrated the shrewd mind behind her small, heart-shaped face.

"To avoid any potential difficulties, we'll want to meet with the INS. We also want to have our attorney look over the temporary guardianship papers."

"Yes, of course."

"And I'll need a crash course in sign language, so I can understand Paulo's needs."

"We can arrange that, as well."

"This is all dependent on Paulo wanting to stay with us," Deb conceded, recognizing that the issue of temporary custody was far from decided. "He might not take to a family as noisy and lively as ours."

"I don't think that will be a problem," Janice said, truly relaxing for the first time since she'd learned the couple who'd applied to adopt Paulo had hit the divorce courts. "He was a godsend at the mission, helping us with the other kids."

"Then I guess the next step is for me to meet him."

When she planted both hands on the arms of her chair and would have levered herself up, Cari waved her back. "Stay put. I'll go get him."

She made her way down the hall, both relieved and regretful that Paulo would have to make yet another wrenching transition before he gained a sense of permanence and stability.

The door to Mac's room stood partway open. She heard the unmistakable sound of canned laughter coming from the TV and rapped twice before poking her head inside.

"Mac?"

He was stretched out on the bed, sound asleep despite the raucous cartoon on the TV. His blue hospital pajamas were gone, traded for cutoffs and a gray USMC sweatshirt with the arms ripped out. The sickly pallor that had tinged his face after the loss of so much blood had disappeared as well. Cari's glance lingered on the sling and bandages strapping his right arm to his chest before drifting to the boy curled up at his good side.

Paulo was zonked out, too. His dark head lay tucked right next to Mac's chin. He wore his favorite Spider-Man T-shirt, of course. Janice had confessed that she washed it out for him every evening.

A little ache started in Cari's chest and spread to her throat. The thought flashed into her head that here was her family, ready-made and waiting. Just as quickly, she pushed it out again. She couldn't let herself start weaving fantasies like that. Not yet, anyway. They all faced too many uncertainties at this point, not the least of which was whether Mac reciprocated this confused feeling Cari was becoming more convinced by the moment was love.

Extracting the TV remote from Mac's slack grip, she clicked off the cartoons. ''Hey, you two,'' she said in the blessed quiet that followed. ''Wake up.''

Mac pried up one eyelid, then the other. ''Aren't you supposed to wake your sleeping prince with a kiss?''

''You're not real up on your fairy tales, are you? The prince is the one who wakes up Sleeping Beauty.''

''Hey, I'm easy. Either way works for me.''

Cari grinned, but the realization that Paulo had blinked awake and was listening to the silly exchange kept her from accommodating Mac's wishes right then and there.

''No time for fairy tales right now. You two need to haul your buns out of bed and come meet my sister.''

''She's here?''

''Yep. With a promise to take Paulo to the fast-food joint of his choice while they get to know one another.''

''Hear that, kid? You can have your pick. Pizza, tacos or hamburgers.''

His brow knitting, the boy eased upright, but the magic last word killed his scowl before it could fully form. He signed something neither Mac nor Cari could interpret. Impatient, he shaped a high arch with his hands.

"That didn't take long," Mac said, laughing. "One trip to McDonald's and you're already hooked. Come on, kid, let's go meet Lieutenant Dunn's sister."

Mac swung his feet off the bed. The rest of him followed without so much as a wince, Cari noted. The man was leather tough, she thought with a stab of admiration that got all mixed up with greedy hunger when he maneuvered into a pair of black rubber flip-flops. His cutoffs ended about midway down hard, muscled thighs. The ragged armhole his gray sweat-shirt afforded a tantalizing glimpse of more male flesh.

As they exited the room and started down the hall, Paulo's hand slipped into Mac's. The boy would never admit it, Cari was sure, but he had to be scared. Once again his world was about to shift around him.

Deb, bless her, knew exactly how to ease his fears. She sent Mac a curious glance, but focused her warm smile on the boy. "Hello, Paulo. I'm Deb. I'm hoping you'll come and stay with me and my family for a while. I should warn you, though, we have two dogs. Big dogs. And two cats. Here, I'll show you a picture."

Janice said something quietly in Caribe. The boy edged closer to Deb's chair. His expression remained wary as she pulled out the photos she'd brought.

"The one with the curly hair is Pierre the Poodle. The one with the dirty face is my son Ben. He's about your age and heavy into action figures. He sent one for you, as a welcome gift."

She delved into her tote again and produced a plastic, lizard-headed toy.

"This is Darcon. Or Dracon. I'm not sure which. He's for you," she prompted, holding out the figure.

Paulo glanced at Janice, who signaled he should accept the gift. He played with the movable arms and legs for a moment, then tucked the figure against his side and flashed a quick sign.

"He says thank you."

"You're welcome," Deb returned. "I'm sorry I can't understand sign language. I'm going to learn, though. Will you help me?"

Paulo's quick nod led to another warm smile and more photos. Fifteen minutes later the boy left with Deb, Janice and the dapper church official to find the closest hamburger joint. Harry White departed for another session with the attorney the church had flown in, leaving Mac and Cari alone for the first time since those quiet hours just before dawn in Caribe.

The memory of how they'd killed those hours started a tight curl of desire deep in her belly. Mac's edgy restlessness when faced with the prospect of going back to his room had her suggesting an alternative.

"If Nurse Ratchet gets an okay from your docs, are you ready to blow this joint for a few hours?"

"More than ready."

"Let me go talk to her."

Nurse Ratchet, otherwise known as Lieutenant Commander Smallwood, got the okay.

"Dr. Atwater agrees it'll do the major good to get away from here for a while," she related, her glance on the tall, tanned marine at the far end of the hall. "He wants to talk to him in the morning, though."

The guarded note in her voice brought Cari's head around. "Has he heard from the orthopedic surgeons about Mac's shoulder replacement?"

The lieutenant commander hesitated. "From one of them."

She wouldn't say more. She didn't have to. Cari walked back down the hall praying that the second specialist would offer a different assessment of Mac's candidacy for replacement surgery.

Twenty minutes later, she parked her rental car outside a waterfront restaurant that advertised the meanest crabs in south Texas.

Chapter 11

"I like your sister," Mac confided over a late lunch of steamed crab and fried clams.

"You'll like her even more after you see her in action." Smiling, Cari dunked a clam in creamy tartar sauce. "Deb swears she could never take the discipline of military life, yet somehow manages to get her kids off to school, the dogs and cats to the vet and her husband on his way to work each morning wearing a silly grin."

"A four-star general in the making," Mac agreed.

"My whole family is like that. I don't ever remember my mom raising her voice to us kids—and I know we gave her plenty of opportunity—but she kept the troops in line."

"Must be where you inherited it," he commented. "You've got a core of solid steel inside that pint-sized package."

"That's a compliment, right?"

She was never quite sure with Mac.

"That's most definitely a compliment." Smiling, he wrapped his fist around a giant-sized mug of iced tea. "If your sister has half your bullheaded determination to see things through, she's a remarkable woman."

Her skin warmed with pleasure. The flush added to the heat generated by the sight of Mac downing a long swallow of his tea. She found her glance riveted to the strong column of his throat, the smooth play of muscle and tendon, the beginnings of a five o'clock shadow darkening the underside of his chin. Suddenly, she ached to rub her cheek against his, to enjoy the scratchy contact.

One lascivious thought led instantly to another. In the blink on an eye, she was imagining how it would feel to rub areas other than his cheek. Heat speared through her, and the muscles low in her belly spasmed.

"What about you?" she asked, as much to recover from the sudden wallop as to keep the conversation rolling. "Any brothers or sisters?"

"None that I know of, although…"

"Although?"

"My mother departed the scene when I was about ten. For all I know, she could have produced a whole passel of additional offspring."

"What about your dad?"

"He departed shortly after that."

His tone was easy, but Cari sensed the walls going up. This time, she decided to go around them.

"So who raised you?"

"A series of foster families."

He deflected her rush of pity with a wry smile.

"I wasn't the easiest kid to take in. Like your sister, I had a distinct aversion to discipline."

"Uh-huh. That's why you chose the U.S. Marine Corps."

The smile deepened. "It was either the marines or jail. For once, I made the right choice. Looks like you need a refill on your iced tea."

With that neat change of subject, he turned and signaled the waiter. The windows behind him were hooked up to allow the breeze from the Gulf to skip through the restaurant, fluttering the paper napkins. The late-afternoon sun bounced off the water in a thousand sparkling pinpricks and framed Mac in a nimbus of light. Another wave of heat washed over Cari again as she took in the rugged masculinity of his profile.

Her glance slid down to the bandages encasing his shoulder. She had no idea how much pain he was experiencing, if any. The nurses had told her he'd stopped taking the pain medication two days ago and refused so much as an aspirin to get him through the past few nights.

It was the night ahead that occupied her thoughts.

"How's your shoulder?" she asked when they departed the Crab Shack and made for her rented vehicle.

"It's there."

"Are you in a hurry to get back to the hospital?"

"What do you think?"

"What I think," she said, sliding into the driver's seat, "is that it's still early. Why don't we detour by the visiting officers' quarters? You can take a look at the final draft of the report," she added conversationally. "I have it on my laptop."

Cari let him go on thinking she had work on her mind until the door snicked shut behind them. She leaned against it, intending to inform him her intentions were somewhat less than honorable.

She never got the chance.

Mac's intentions evidently ran along the same lines as hers. He propped his good arm against the door, leaned his body into hers and swooped in for a kiss that knocked the breath back down her throat.

"So I guess you're not interested in the draft report," she teased when they both came up for air.

"Not as interested as I am in the buttons on this shirt," he replied, zeroing in on her red-checkered blouse.

One by one, the buttons gave under his fingers. Shivers danced just under Cari's skin as his knuckles traced a path from her neckline to her waist. One-handed, he shoved the material aside. When his breath left on a long hiss, she gave silent thanks that she'd opted for a lacy bra and high-on-the-thigh bikini briefs this morning instead of her usual cotton and spandex.

"If you hadn't suggested coming back to your quarters," he growled, his palm hot on the soft mound of her flesh, "I was going to prop a chair under the door handle of my hospital room and ravage you."

"You've been wounded in the line of duty. How about I do the ravishing this time around?"

His hand stilled. Eyes glinting, he gave her a wolf-ish grin. "Works for me."

"Okay, Major. The first step is to get you semi-horizontal."

Hooking two fingers in the waistband of his cut-offs, she tugged him to the sofa.

"Sit!"

"Yes, ma'am."

He lowered himself to the sofa and watched with interest as she unzipped her slacks. They slithered down her hips, landed in a heap on the carpet. She stepped out of them and undid the last few buttons on her blouse. It followed her slacks to the floor. Yanking at the clip that held her hair up in a loose twist, she shook the thick brown strands free. A moment later she'd kicked off her sandals, planted a knee on either side of Mac's hips and straddled him.

"This is nice," she observed, brushing his lips with hers. "We're eye to eye and mouth to mouth."

"*Very* nice."

She dropped a string of kisses that trailed from his lips to his chin to the taut cords at the side of his neck. He took advantage of her crouched position to find the curve of her bottom with his good hand.

As he fondled her through the silky fabric of her briefs, fiery hunger ignited in Cari's veins. She wanted to crawl all over him, chew him up and swallow him whole. Nipping at his warm flesh, she issued a husky demand.

"Promise me you'll tell me if I hurt your shoulder."

Mac couldn't help himself. Laughing, he squeezed her butt. "Oh, babe, you've already got me hurting so bad you could sit on my shoulder and I wouldn't feel it."

He slouched against the sofa back, taking her with him. Her tight, trim behind filled his hand. Her breasts brushed his chest. All inclination to laughter fled as

Mac met the thrust of her hot, wet tongue with his own.

He hadn't lied to her. He was hurting from his neck to his knees. Had been, one way or another, since the first time he'd laid eyes on this stubborn, seductive, incredible woman. He'd buried his hunger for her all those weeks in New Mexico. He'd had a job to do. So had she. She'd also been on the phone to that wuss up in Washington almost every night.

That was then, he thought on a surge of desire so hot and raw it seared his entire body. Now...

Now, she was his.

The primitive male urge to possess her, to leave his scent on her, slammed into him. It took him a moment to remember he was a United States Marine, not some Roman mercenary or robber baron who could cart a woman off as plunder. Another moment to admit Cari wasn't the carting-off type. She'd probably deck him if he tried any Neanderthal tactics on her.

Besides, he didn't have a single damned condom anywhere on him!

Cursing his lack of foresight, Mac slid his hand between her thighs. His thumb rubbed back and forth, generating a friction that soon had her gasping and Mac sweating. Gritting his teeth to keep from hooking his arm around her waist and dragging her under him, he found the leg opening of her briefs.

Her inner flesh was smooth and hot. Mac slipped

a finger inside her, then two. With slow, sure thrusts, he stoked the fires that flushed her skin and left it slick and damp. Fierce satisfaction gripped him as Cari's head went back. Writhing, she rode the waves of wild sensation.

Suddenly, she went stiff. Her eyes flew open. "Mac, I'm too… I can't…"

"So don't."

She tried to wiggle away. "I'm supposed to be…doing the rav…aging here."

"We'll take turns."

Ruthlessly suppressing his own raging need, he exerted just enough pressure with his thumb to produce a long, ragged groan. Once more Cari's head went back. Her eyes squeezed shut. Violent shudders racked her small, perfect body.

Mac almost lost it himself right then and there. She was his most erotic fantasy come to life. Slender curves. Hot flesh. Her back arched. Her hair was a spill of dark, tangled silk.

Slowly, her thighs relaxed and she sank down onto his. Mac ground his back teeth together until the last throes of her climax passed and she opened her eyes.

"Wow!" She essayed a wobbly smile. "Give me a minute and I'll take my turn."

Still in the grip of his own aching desire and the primal need to possess this woman, Mac started to tell her he intended to give her a whole lifetime of minutes. Just in time, he bit back the words. He wasn't in any shape to stake that kind of a claim on her. Not yet.

Once the docs fit him with a new shoulder, though, she couldn't run far or fast enough to get away from him. Forcing himself to bide his time—mentally and physically—he stayed perfectly still until Cari had regained enough strength to slide off his lap onto her knees.

With a small, wicked smile, she popped the snap on his cut-offs. The zipper came down. Her hands found him, freed him, gripped him. She trailed the tip of a finger down the rigid shaft. Drew it back up again. Wet her lips.

Then it was Mac's turn to throw his head back and let out a long, low groan.

The rap on the door came while Mac's heart was still trying to pump blood back to his outer extremities. He dragged his head up and rasped out a hoarse query.

"Expecting company?"

"No." She dropped her voice to a husky whisper. "Maybe if we keep real quiet, whoever it is will go away."

The ploy didn't work. Another rap rattled the door, harder this time.

"Hey, Cari!" Dave Scott's deep voice boomed

from the hallway. "I spotted your car in the parking lot. Haul your buns over to the door and open up. I need your chop on the sequence we used to take *Pegasus* from sea to air mode down in Caribe to finalize this report."

Muttering an oath worthy of a true salt, Cari snatched up her blouse and fumbled with the buttons. "Hang on a sec! I'll be right there."

Mac got himself together well before she did. Not surprising, since she'd stripped down to her skivvies and he was still more in than out of his clothes. He pushed off the sofa, then waited until she'd scrambled into her slacks and shoved the shirttails inside the waistband before strolling across the room.

When he opened the door, surprise sent the pilot's sun-bleached blond brows soaring. "McIver! What the heck are you doing out of the hospital?"

Dave's glance winged to Cari, cut back. A delighted grin split his face. "Never mind. I'm a little slow on the uptake sometimes, but this one's a no-brainer."

With a flash of her bright copper hair, Kate poked her head out of the open doorway of the room across the hall. "What's a no-brainer?"

Her green eyes brightened when she saw who Dave was talking to. "Hey, gang, Mac's here."

She came across the hallway, followed in short order by Jill Bradshaw and Doc Richardson. When Captain Westfall appeared at the threshold of the room across the hall, Mac's easy smile slid off his face. Instinctively, he straightened and squared his shoulders. Or tried to. The knifing pain had him biting back a curse and brought Cari instantly to his side.

"At ease, man."

Westfall issued the gruff order, then shifted his gaze to Cari. Despite the calm smile she plastered on her face, he couldn't fail to note the whisker burn reddening her cheeks and chin. Nor could any of the others. Kate shared a look with Jill, while Doc Richardson manfully tried to smother a grin. Captain Westfall, thankfully, ignored the red flags.

"Did they discharge you or did you just decide to go AWOL?" he asked Mac.

"Neither. The doc gave me a few hours' shore leave."

"Good. How about you use what remains of it to go over the final report I'm delivering to the Joint Chiefs of Staff tomorrow?"

"Yes, sir."

"Lieutenant Dunn, we'll need your input as well."

"Of course. I'll be right there."

He turned and retreated into the suite across the hall. The others straggled after him, leaving a rueful Cari to shag a hand through her tangled hair.

"We need to work on our timing," she muttered to Mac. "Seems like every time we get hot and bothered, we wind up with someone shooting at us or the entire test cadre gathered around as interested observers. How's your shoulder?''

He should have known she wouldn't miss his involuntary wince when he tried to go into a brace.

"It's fine," he lied, toeing a bit of plastic out from under the couch. "Is this yours?"

"Yes. Thanks."

While she twisted up her hair and anchored it to the back of her head, Mac slid his feet into his flip-flops. Marginally presentable, they joined the group crowded around a small table in the suite across the hall. Chairs bumped and elbows jostled as the others made room for two more.

"Here you go," Kate said, passing them copies of the report. "The latest version, hot off the press. We've made some changes to the draft you need to take a look at."

The printed pages immediately absorbed Cari. They should have absorbed Mac, too. The report represented the culmination of long months of tests, trials and evaluations. The fact that it might also represent the culmination of his military career carved a small hole in his gut.

He'd demanded and received brutal honesty from the surgeons who'd tried—and failed—to patch together the shattered remnants of his shoulder. The damage to both tissue and bone went beyond their capacity to repair it. In their considered opinion, it went beyond being able to support even an artificial joint. His only hope was that one of the specialists they'd sent his case file to would accept him as a candidate for replacement surgery despite the odds.

The tension Cari had drained from him with her hands and her mouth and her supple, incredible body crept back. The muscles in the back of his neck knotted. His fist tightened on the report. With a silent curse, Mac eased his grip and forced himself to focus on the lines of print.

Forty minutes later, Mac realized this meeting presaged the end of something else, something that seemed to hit each of the officers present when Captain Westfall gave his nod to the last page of the revised report.

"Well, that's it." With careful precision, he aligned the pages. "The analyses we've provided here should give the Joint Chiefs sufficient information to make a go or no-go decision on *Pegasus*."

He slid the thick report into a folder stamped with the appropriate classified markings.

"Jill, I'll leave the draft copies with you to shred and dispose of."

"Yes, sir."

"Dave, I'm relying on you to make sure every system aboard *Pegasus* is thoroughly shaken down before you fly back to New Mexico on Monday."

"Roger that, sir. Neither *Pegasus* nor I will lift off unless I'm confident we can come down again soft and easy."

"Good."

The captain speared a glance at each of his officers.

"Whatever the Joint Chiefs decide, I want you to know I was proud to have you on my team."

This was it. Possibly the last time the Pegasus cadre would work together. The captain and the other five would return to New Mexico to close down test operations. Mac would remain here in Texas until the docs rendered their verdict. The realization that their urgent mission and tight-knit team had both come to an end punched into each of them.

Silence gripped the room. Every officer present knew the usual hearty handshakes and promises to grab a beer the next time their paths crossed wouldn't hack it. But that was the standard formula, one they'd all relied on when readying for the next move to a new duty station. The only one they had to rely on now.

The handshakes were hard. The smiles were warm and genuine. They dispersed with a chorus of promises to gather for the official ceremony marking *Pegasus*'s acceptance as an operational vehicle—whenever and wherever that might occur.

* * *

A pensive silence filled the rental car as Cari drove Mac back to the hospital. After the searing intimacy of their stolen hours together, they now had to factor a pending separation and Mac's uncertain future into their still tenuous relationship.

At Mac's insistence, Cari pulled up to the front of the hospital. "We have the rest of the weekend," she reminded him when he reached across his strapped arm to open the passenger door. "All day tomorrow and Sunday. I want you to meet Jack, Deb's husband, and their kids. Maybe we could spring you loose again tomorrow morning. We'll have a picnic on the beach with Paulo and the whole gang."

"Sounds good."

He made an effort to sound enthusiastic. She knew how much he must hate the thought of being left to twiddle his thumbs when the rest of the cadre dispersed. She also noted the white lines that bracketed his mouth. He'd need more than an aspirin to get through tonight, she guessed.

Her rush of guilt at pushing him to his physical limits got all mixed up with an urge to cradle him in her arms and soothe away his pain.

She lifted a hand to stroke his cheek. Mac caught it in his and tugged her close. Forcing a smile, he dropped a hard kiss on her mouth.

"See you tomorrow, beautiful."

Chapter 12

Cari arrived at the hospital just past ten the following morning. The dazzling sunshine of the previous day had given way to gray, sullen skies and a stiff breeze off the Gulf that carried a definite nip to it. Shivering in her lightweight chinos and daffodil-yellow cotton drifter, she hurried across the parking lot.

They'd have to revise their plans for a picnic on the beach with Deb and Jack and the kids, she thought. Go for some kind of indoor activity instead.

Instantly, her thoughts zipped back to the indoor activity she and Mac had indulged in the evening before. A rush of heat warmed her skin, countering the goose bumps raised by the breeze. She still couldn't quite believe she'd jumped Mac's bones the way she had. Or that he'd turned the tables on her so skillfully. Using only one arm, he'd managed to dissolve her into a shivering puddle of ecstasy. She could just imagine the magic he would work on her eager body when he regained full use of his other arm.

If he regained full use of that arm.

The distinct possibility he might not took some of the spring from her step. The little he'd told her about himself yesterday confirmed her suspicion the corps was more than just Russ McIver's career. It was his life.

Well, if the worst happened, they'd just have to come up with a strategy to deal with it. Mac wasn't the kind to sit around and feel sorry for himself. Nor would Cari let him. They'd get through this together.

It wasn't until she was in the elevator, stabbing the button for the fourth floor, that Cari realized she was now thinking in plurals. *They* would have to come up with a strategy. *They* would get through this.

Sometime during the night she'd taken that next step. From wondering if she and Mac could carve a future out of the uncertainties facing them, she was now determined to make it happen.

Impatient now, she waited for the elevator doors to whir open and hurried down the hall. When she reached Mac's room, the door was open. The bed was neatly made, sheets turned down and tucked in at sharp angles. Its occupant stood at the window. He was in uniform—green gabardine trousers, precisely aligned brass belt buckle, tailored khaki shirt with gleaming insignia and rows of bright, colorful ribbons. Even the blue sling strapping his arm tight against his chest was perfectly squared.

Her heart skipped happily at seeing him standing tall even as a tiny thread of worry snaked along her veins. She could think of only one reason for him to be in uniform.

"Hello, Mac."

Her suspicion was confirmed when he turned his head. He arranged his expression into a welcoming smile, but Cari could see he had to work at it.

"What's with the khakis?" she asked, although she could pretty well guess the answer.

"The docs made their rounds earlier. They're discharging me."

Skirting the bed, she joined him at the wide window. The storm clouds piling up over the Gulf seemed an appropriate background for the news Mac delivered in a carefully neutral tone.

"The surgeon says he can't do anything more for me. Nor can either of the civilian specialists he consulted, it turns out."

"Well, hell!"

His smile almost reached his eyes. "That pretty well sums up my sentiments, too."

She ached for him, for the hope that was now smashed along with tendon and bone and muscle.

"Your arm's a long way from healed. Surely the doc's not sending you back to duty?"

"He's putting me on restricted duty until the bones knit as best they can and I complete a regimen of physical therapy."

"Then you'll meet a medical evaluation board."

It wasn't a question. Cari understood the process as well as Mac did. Nodding, he sidestepped the unsure future to focus on the immediate.

"I called Captain Westfall this morning and caught him as he was leaving for D.C. He agrees with the docs that I should ship back to my home station at Cherry Point to begin the physical therapy."

That made sense. The dispensary at the Pegasus site wasn't equipped for the kind of therapy Mac would require. Still, the knowledge that a half a continent would soon separate them carved a little hole in Cari's heart.

She'd known it was coming. With the Pegasus project winding down, the entire team would soon disperse to their various home stations. They'd pretty well said their unofficial farewells after the meeting last night. She wasn't ready to let go yet, though. Not of this particular member of the team, anyway.

"You don't have to leave today, do you?"

Mac hesitated. The docs had urged him to take some time off and fully regain his strength before going back to his duty station. Captain Westfall had echoed the recommendation, but understood Mac's need to focus on something, *anything,* other than the black hole that used to be his career.

It yawned under his feet now, threatening to sink more than his military career. If he wasn't damned careful, it would swallow Cari, too.

"Stay the weekend," she urged softly. "With me."

He wanted to. God knew, he wanted to! He'd spent most of last night alternating between the grinding ache in his shoulder and the far fiercer ache stirred by the mere thought of this woman. Every time he'd closed his eyes, he'd see her. Her head thrown back, her hair a tangled tumble, her sleek, supple body shuddering in glorious release.

Along with that erotic vision came vivid reminders of how she'd used her hands and her mouth and her teeth to bring him to the same shattering state. Just the memory was enough to put Mac into a sweat.

It also made him crave more than her hands and her mouth and her teeth. He wanted all of her. Under him. Around him. All over him. But not for a hurried few hours. In the dark moments just before dawn, he'd realized he wanted to wake up to Cari's hair spread across his pillow. To share the first cup of coffee with her in the morning and drift off to sleep with her body tucked tight against his at night.

He'd believed he had a shot at fulfilling one or all of those cravings until the surgeon delivered his news this morning.

"I'm not sure spending the weekend together is such a good idea," he said quietly. "Maybe it's better to make the break now, before either of us gets in too deep."

He expected the words to produce an argument, maybe anger. Quite possibly an aching sense of loss that mirrored his own. What he didn't expect was her snort of laughter. Taken completely aback, he stared down at the amusement dancing in her eyes.

"Nice try, McIver. We both know it's too late for a clean break. We're already in too deep. The question now is what the dickens we're going to do about it."

"Cari…"

She cut him off with an airy wave of one hand. "This isn't the time or the place to decide that question. You're coming with me, mister."

Mac thought about reminding her that he outranked her and should be the one issuing the orders. That he needed to confirm his travel arrangements back to Cherry Point. That a few more hours wouldn't change the situation. With a spurt of greedy selfishness, he kept his jaw clamped shut while Cari dumped his few personal items into the plastic tote bag the nursing aide had provided for that purpose.

Almost shaking with a combination of bravado and relief, Cari kept her back to him as she scooped up razor, shaving cream, soap, deodorant, toothbrush and toothpaste. Her laughing comeback had thrown him completely off balance, but he wouldn't remain off balance for long. He'd challenge her blithe assertion they were both already in too deep. Do his best to convince her they should back off. Probably suggest they wait until time and distance and the results of the medical board had added perspective to their situation.

Well, she wasn't backing off. Not now, and not any time in the foreseeable future. What's more, she fully intended to use the next forty-eight hours to storm the citadel of Mac's heart in pretty much the same manner the marines had once stormed the halls of Montezuma.

Her resolve firming with every second, she tossed in his shorts, sweatshirt and skivvies, along with his rubber flip-flops. The neatly folded hospital pajamas she ignored. If matters progressed as she intended them to, Mac wouldn't need them.

The plastic bag bulged at the sides by the time she'd finished. She swept a last look around. "Do I have all the essentials?"

When he hesitated for several long moments, Cari drew in a deep breath. She didn't want to discuss their future in the hospital. She'd prefer to have him away from the scent of antiseptic and shiny, squeaky tiled floors when they talked about what came next. She'd lay her feelings out here if she had to, though.

Before she could fully marshal her arguments, Mac spiked them by moving to the wood-grained metal cabinet beside the bed and extracting a small paper sack. With a wry grin, he tossed it her way.

"*Now* you have all the essentials."

Curious, she snuck a peek at the box inside the sack. The box of condoms kicked her pulse into immediate overdrive, and laughter once again danced in her eyes.

"Think we'll need an entire dozen?"

Mac's answering smile melted her insides. "A man can only hope. I was caught unprepared last time. This time, we'll do things right."

She led the way out of his room, fervently wishing she hadn't committed to spending a portion of their precious remaining hours with Deb and her noisy, lively brood.

When Cari called ahead to advise her sister they were on the way, Deb suggested an indoor pizza and game fest as an alternative to their planned picnic.

Evidently the rented condo came equipped with a large selection of board games.

Rain had begun to lash the Gulf by the time Cari and Mac pulled up at the beachside condo. Spray flew up from the gray sea in lacy spumes. Waves rolled and crashed on the beach. Thinking Mac might want to change out of his uniform, Cari grabbed the plastic sack and made a dash for the condo. Mac followed hard on her heels.

Her brother-in-law answered the door and attempted to make himself heard over the shrieks of laughter and rafter-rattling barks emanating from the living room.

"Jack Hamilton, Major." Out of consideration for Mac's injured right arm he didn't offer to shake hands. "Glad I finally get to meet you. From the way Paulo perks up whenever your name is mentioned, it's obvious you're his hero."

"I don't know about the hero part, but we have become pals. He's a good kid."

When he wasn't beaning marines in the head with rocks, Cari thought wryly.

"Sorry 'bout the noise," Jack apologized as he led the way inside. "Deb's doing her best to keep the kids entertained until the storm passes."

"It might not blow over until tomorrow," Cari warned as he led the way into the living room. "Kate—our associate from the National Oceanic and

Atmospheric Administration—says the front has settled over this corner of the Gulf.''

Jack didn't seem to find the prospect of being cooped up in a small condo with a pregnant wife, five children and an eighty-pound poodle the least daunting. That was only one of the reasons Cari loved him. The goofy smile that came over his face when his glance rested on Deb was another.

Her sister sat at the table set strategically near the sliding glass with their panoramic view of the Gulf. Her youngest was nestled against her distended belly. The rest of her brood were in chairs crowded around the table.

''Thank goodness!'' Deb exclaimed when she spotted the newcomers. ''Reinforcements! Grab a chair and help me fight off this hoard of warlocks.''

''Not warlocks, Mom.'' His eyes serious behind his round, Harry Potter-style glasses, her eight-year-old corrected her. ''Wizards.''

''Right. Wizards. Major, this is our eldest, Ben.'' She gave each of the kids crowded around the table a quick nod. ''In order of age but not importance, these are Julie, Logan and Pitty-Pat, also known as Patricia. Paulo you already know, of course.''

From her precarious perch on her mother's almost nonexistent lap, two-year-old Pitty-Pat thrust her thumb in her mouth and regarded Mac with wide

brown eyes. He returned her solemn look before
knuckling Paulo's dark head.

"Hiya, kid."

The boy tried for one of his scowls at this rough
and ready treatment, but couldn't quite disguise his
relief at seeing a familiar face. He settled back in his
chair, making no effort to shrug off the hand Mac
rested on his shoulder while the older kids peppered
the newcomer with questions about the badges and
ribbons adorning his uniform shirt.

"Are you in the coast guard like Aunt Cari?"

"What's that shiny metal thing?"

"Do you know how to navigate by the stars?"

The last came from Ben, who, his father explained,
was working on a merit badge for scouts on celestial
navigation.

"I'm in the United States Marine Corps," he answered with an easy smile, "not the coast guard. This
is an expert marksmanship badge. And yes, I can find
my way using celestial navigation but prefer to use
GPS."

"Then you should be really good at hunting down
witches and wizards," Deb said cheerfully. "Here,
take my place. I need to make a potty run."

"Again?"

"Mo...om!"

From the groans that rose from the group at the
table, this wasn't her first potty run of the game. Nor,

Cari suspected, would it be her last. Unperturbed, Deb shifted Pitty-Pat off her lap onto the one next to hers, which happened to be Paulo's. The toddler went willingly, and the boy caged his arms around her with the same casually protective air he'd used with little Rosa.

Jack dragged a chair in from the living room for Cari and wedged it in next to the one Deb had turned over to Mac. She took it willingly, but wouldn't let them abandon the game in progress to start over and include her.

"I'll just watch while you finish this game."

Jack and Ben did their best to explain the complex and apparently fluid rules of engagement to Mac, Deb's stand-in. To Cari's amusement, the marine was soon racing for his life through nests of giant spiders and smacking into castle walls that inexplicably moved when he did. After his third encounter with one of these board-jumping walls, even Paulo was chuffing with laughter.

"Think that's funny, do you?" Mac rattled the dice. "Better watch it, kid. I'm hot on your tail and coming after you."

The noise levels rose with each roll of the dice. Squeals of delight, shrieks of dismay, exclamations of triumph all reverberated through the condo. Pierre the Poodle added to the pandemonium by dashing back and forth. Torn between the action at the table and his self-appointed duty of warning off the pesky sea-gulls swooping down outside, he •emitted nonstop growls, yips and woofs.

Despite the pandemonium, Cari found herself wishing the game would go on forever. This was what she wanted. For herself *and* for Mac. A noisy room filled with love and laughter and children. All happy, all giggling. Swallowing the lump in her throat, she took in the sight of Mac and Paulo trading mock scowls while engaged in seemingly mortal combat.

Deb returned from the bathroom, but waved Mac back when he would have relinquished her place at the board. "You're doing great. Keep rolling those dice and I'll order the pizza. Who wants what on theirs?"

She noted the long list of particulars with the mental agility of a waitress and ambled into the kitchen. Cari abandoned her observation post to join her. Thankfully, the swinging door to the kitchen cut the noise level from ultra high frequency decibel level to almost bearable.

"I don't know how you maintain your calm in the midst of all that chaos," Cari commented with a wry smile.

Laughing, Deb dragged the fat local phone book out of the drawer under the wall-mounted phone. "The same way you maintain yours when you take your coast guard cutter out in near gale-force winds to chase down some dope smuggler.''

Pizza ordered, the two sisters set out soft drinks and plastic cups, then claimed the rattan bar stools set at the kitchen counter. With their backs to the swinging door and a view through the windows over the sink of the storm-tossed Gulf before them, they stole a few moments of relative calm and comfort.

''I like your major,'' Deb commented while waiting for the fizz in her soft drink to subside.

''Funny, he said exactly the same thing about you.''

''What's funny about that? He's obviously a man of discerning taste and unerring judgment. But then we already knew that. He hooked you, didn't he?''

''Yeah,'' Cari admitted softly. ''He did.''

''So what's the deal with you two? When are you going to take him home to meet the folks?''

She answered the easier question first. ''Not any time soon. The docs are sending him back to his duty station on restricted duty while he completes a regimen of physical therapy.''

Deb's brow knit. ''They're not going to do that shoulder replacement you told me about?''

''Apparently he's not a viable candidate.''

''Bummer!'' She digested that for a few moments. ''Back to the first part of my question. What's the deal with you two?''

"There is no deal. Yet. The surgeons just delivered the bad news this morning. Mac and I haven't had a chance to talk about where we go from here."

"What's to talk about? It's obvious you're crazy about him. If the feeling's mutual, why don't you just go for it?"

"That's pretty much my plan, but it's not as simple as it sounds. Mac has to return to the marine corps base at Cherry Point, North Carolina, for one thing. I'm heading off in a different direction. For another, he won't know whether he'll remain on active duty until after he meets a medical evaluation board."

"I don't see the problem. You love him. You think he loves you. You should do what comes naturally and work through the problems as they come."

Leave it to Deb to strip matters down to basics. Her husband and her family came first. Everything else came a distant second.

"Besides which," she added, "that boy needs a home. A permanent home."

"Paulo?"

"Yes, Paulo. Don't tell me you haven't thought about adopting him. I saw the way you watched him and Mac together. You want the whole package, sister mine. I could read it in your face."

"Yes, I do. But it can't happen, Deb. Not any time in the foreseeable future, anyway. My duties take me away for long stretches at a time. Mac is facing months of painful therapy before he meets that eval board. The therapy could take months, even years. No court is going to grant us custody of a child under those conditions. Particularly when the child himself may have to undergo a series of operations.''

Deb's jaw locked in stubborn lines. She wasn't about to concede the point, but had trouble coming up with cogent counterarguments. Absorbed in the discussion, neither sister noticed the boy who'd nudged the swinging door open a few inches, an empty glass in his hand.

His young face twisted into an expression too old for his age. As silent as a shadow, he backed out of the kitchen.

Chapter 13

The battle of the boards carried over until the doorbell buzzed. Instantly, the kids lost all interest in witches and wizards.

"Pizza!" five-year-old Logan shouted.

"Peasa!" Pitty-Pat echoed joyfully.

"Okay, kids." Their father shoved back his chair. "You know the drill."

Mac watched the resulting scramble with an appreciative eye. The Hamilton clan could have shown a platoon of new recruits a thing or two. With a furious burst of energy, Ben and Julie cleared the table and put away the board game. Logan dashed into the kitchen to help his mom and aunt Cari bring in plastic plates and drinking glasses. Pitty-Pat's chubby fingers curled around Paulo's to draw him into the whirlwind of activity.

"I show you."

His mouth set, Paulo jerked his hand free. The toddler's face screwed up for a moment but she was too well used to the vagaries of older siblings to make a fuss. Curling her rosebud lips around her thumb, she trotted off.

Mac noted the exchange. He also noted that Jack was reaching for his wallet. "Lunch is on me," he said easily, dropping a hand on Paulo's shoulder. "Come on, squirt. Help me carry in the pizza."

The deliveryman was huddled under the skimpy front overhang. Rain splashed off his red carrying case onto the cardboard boxes Mac piled in Paulo's outstretched arms. He gave the man a generous tip for braving the weather and closed the door on the storm.

When Paulo started for the living room, Mac stayed him with a gentle hand. "You okay, kid?"

The boy's eyes lifted. Mac caught a flash of something he couldn't interpret in their dark depths. Frowning, he eased the boxes out of Paulo's hands onto a handy hall table and dropped down on one knee.

"What is it? Why did you suddenly get so quiet in the middle of the game?"

Paulo hesitated, then used his hands in an attempt to communicate. Frustrated by his inability to understand, Mac shook his head. "Sorry, I don't get what you're saying."

Scowling, the kid reached out and lightly touched his sling.

"Are you worried about my shoulder?"

Paulo answered with a quick jerk of his chin.

"I won't lie to you. It hurts like hell, but it'll get better. Eventually."

The boy's fingers fluttered upward, dusted over the gold oak leaf on the collar of Mac's khaki shirt.

"What?"

Small white teeth bit down on a lower lip. Once more Paulo fingered the oak leaf, this time with an urgent question in his eyes.

Hell! The kid had picked up more than Mac had realized during his visits to the hospital.

"Did you hear I might get booted out of the marines?"

The nod was slower this time.

"Well, I might. But not for a long time yet. They're going to make me do some exercises for a while, see how the shoulder works before they make any decisions."

The urgency faded from the black eyes. It was replaced by something that hovered between resignation and despair. His thin shoulders sagging under the Spi-der-Man T-shirt, he reached for the pizza boxes.

"Listen to me, kid." Curling his good hand under Paulo's chin, he tipped the small face to his. "I know you've got some tough times ahead, too."

Tough didn't begin to describe it. Mac knew all too well what it was like to move into a strange house and try to fit in with a new family, all the while know-ing both were only temporary.

Added to that, the kid faced the possibility of a series of operations followed by the excruciating ex-perience of learning to speak through an artificial voice box. Mac decided right then and there that wherever he was, whatever private hell he might be going through himself, he'd be there when the kid went under the knife.

"I'm going to talk to the Hamiltons. Ask them to keep me posted on how you're doing. I'll talk to you, too. Regularly. And if you decide to have the opera-tion Dr. White told you about, I'll fly in to be with you. I promise."

Paulo didn't believe him. Mac could see it in the kid's expression. He'd been abandoned too many times to pin his hopes on anyone but himself.

Not for the first time Mac cursed the bullet that had landed him in this frigging state of limbo. He couldn't plan, couldn't act, couldn't direct the course of his own life much less affect anyone else's. Savagely, he

shoved aside his crazy, half-baked idea of standing
sponsor to the kid and sharing a hospital room while
the docs gave Paulo an artificial voice and Mac a new
shoulder. The shoulder wasn't going to happen, but
he'd damned well go AWOL if necessary to hear the
kid speak his first words.

"I'll be there," he promised again. "When you go
into the hospital or any other time you need me. You
just have the Hamiltons call, okay? One call and I'll
hotfoot it down to Shreveport. Got that?"

Paulo nodded but wouldn't meet Mac's eyes. Re-
trieving the pizzas, he carted them into the other
room.

Coming on top of the grim verdict on his shoulder,
Mac's inability to offer the boy more than promises
frayed the edges of his temper. The easy smile stayed
on his face. He downed his share of pizza. He even
managed to hold his own against Pitty-Pat and Logan
in a rowdy game of Mr. Potato Head. But he was
coiled as tight as a cocked pistol by the time Cari told
her sister they had to leave. Although the kids raised
an instant chorus of protests, Deb didn't try to strong-
arm them into staying. Mac got the distinct impression Cari had indicated the two of them needed to
talk.

Talking wasn't the only item on his agenda. Nor
was it the first. The need to tumble this woman into

his arms and into bed grew with each whishing roll of the car's tires on the rain-soaked pavement.

His rational mind said he should put the skids on. Now. Despite Cari's assertion that they were already in too deep, he knew he could slice through the web of desire they'd woven around themselves. One swift cut, that's all it would take to sever the silken ties. Then all he'd have to do was get through the months and years ahead knowing he'd shoved the one woman he'd ever wanted in his life right out of it.

Not that Cari was the type to let a man shove her in *or* out of anything. She had her own agenda, Mac discovered when they dashed through the rain and gained the dry warmth of her rooms at the visiting officers' quarters. An agenda that didn't rank discussing their future within the top two must-do's.

Her first priority, she informed him on a husky note that put an instant kink in his gut, was to get them both naked. Her second, using up the contents of that box of condoms.

She set about the first task almost as soon as the door thudded shut behind them. Her hands eager, she tugged his shirt free of his pants and worked the buttons. As each button slipped through the hole she treated him to nipping little kisses.

Mac held back, reminding himself of all the reasons they should talk before making use of his emergency supplies. Cari's tongue and busy little hands torpedoed the last of his rapidly disintegrating restraint. She got his shirt down his good arm, but the sling stymied her.

"How the heck do you get your clothes on and off over this thing?"

His mouth curved. "Very carefully."

Unbuckling the sling, he eased down the straps. He ignored his shoulder's instant scream of protest and kept his arm bent. Frowning in concentration, Cari carefully removed his uniform blouse and undershirt. They hit the floor while Mac rebuckled the sling.

"You're pretty good with that left hand," she observed, trailing her fingertips down his sternum. As light as it was, her touch set every one of his nerves jumping like sailors on a hot steel deck. And when her fingers slid inside his belt, he gave up any thought of postponing the inevitable.

He wanted this woman with a hunger that gored a hole right through his middle. The flush of desire staining her cheeks told him she wanted him with the same vicious need.

"Come into the bedroom with me," he said on a low growl, "and I'll show you just how good I am with my left hand."

He was better than good, Cari thought on a rush of heat some moments later. He gave a whole new meaning to the term *ambidextrous*.

Wedging pillows under his injured shoulder, he propped himself up enough to explore her sprawled body. He took his time about it. Skimming his left hand from her neck to her knees, he traced every curve, every valley. The calluses on his palm raised little pinpricks of sensation everywhere they brushed. The lazy circle his thumb rasped over her nipple drew it into a tight, tingling bud.

Within moments he'd progressed from her breast to the curve of her belly. When he slid his hand between her thighs and pressed the heel against her mound, Cari shot straight from tiny pinpricks to giant waves of pleasure. Her belly clenched. The sensations piled up, receded, came crashing in again like the surf pounding the south Texas coast. She arched up, careful not to jar his shoulder, and locked her mouth on his.

His hand pressed harder, his fingers probed deeper. Cari teetered on the edge and pulled back only by a sheer effort of will.

"We took turns last time," she panted. "Let's do this together this time."

More than willing, he rolled onto his back and fumbled for his stash of emergency supplies. Cari usually made it a point to take the necessary precautions herself, but the fact that Mac would put her protection before his pleasure melted her heart and left her swimming in a puddle of want.

This task he couldn't manage one-handed, though. Grinning at his muttered curse, she leaned across him and made short work of the foil wrapper. Her hands slow, her smile wicked, she rolled the thin sheath down his rigid, straining length.

Her smile stayed in place until she'd straddled him. It slipped a little as he positioned himself, and disappeared completely when he flexed his thighs and drove upward. Gasping, Cari fell forward and planted her hands on either side of his head.

Her climax came too fast, too hard, too damned soon! Groaning against Mac's mouth, she clenched her muscles and rode the wild, tossing waves. He tangled his hand in her hair, kept her mouth hard on his and flexed his thighs again. A moment later, he followed her over the edge.

If the first time was hard and fast, the second was slow and sweet.

They more or less drifted into it. She was sprawled facedown on the tangled covers, still lazy with pleasure, when he padded in from the bathroom. She watched him with the one eye she didn't have buried in the pillow.

Russ McIver in uniform epitomized today's modern, highly skilled warrior. Out of it, he was all sleek muscle and satisfied male. His weight set the mattress springs creaking as he settled beside her and nuzzled her neck.

"Mmm. That's nice."

"We need to talk, Cari."

"I know. Could you do that a little lower?"

Nuzzling soon gave way to nipping. The bristly rasp of his five o'clock shadow added to the scrape of his teeth. Cari had come fully alive again when she felt a suspicious prod at her backside. Twisting, she aimed a laughing look over her shoulder.

"You certainly recharge your batteries faster than *Pegasus* does."

Grinning at the compliment, he proceeded to demonstrate several other areas in which his performance exceeded that of an all-weather, all-terrain attack/assault vehicle.

By the time they finished, late afternoon had darkened into stormy night and Cari was limp with pleasure. Mac, on the other hand, appeared remarkably together for a man who'd already made a serious dent in his emergency supplies. Hooking his left elbow under his head, he smiled across the pillow at her.

"Have I told you what a remarkable woman you are, Lieutenant Dunn?"

"Not lately." She thought about it for a moment. "Not ever, as a matter of fact. Nor, I would like to point out, have you told me you love me."

He blinked in surprise. "Sure I have."

"Is that right?" Dragging the sheet up, she tucked it under her arms. "When?"

"What, you want the exact time and place?" He searched his memory. "That night in Caribe, after you told me you'd called things off with Jerry-boy. I told you then I had it bad for you."

"Actually, your exact phrasing was that you had the hots for me."

One corner of his mouth tipped up. "That's pretty much the equivalent of saying I love you in marine-speak."

"Not in coast guard lingo. Say it, Mac. I want to hear the words."

His smile took on a curve that was tender and tough and rueful all at the same time. "I love you, Cari. I have from the first time you squared up to me and suggested I get my head out of my butt, or words to that effect."

Snuggling closer, she bent an elbow on his chest and propped her chin in the crook. Her heart was in her eyes as she answered the question in his.

"I love you, too, big guy. So much I was prepared to use your sling to tie you to this bed until you admitted the feeling was mutual."

"Well, damn! I didn't know you were into kinky stuff. It's still not too late for ropes and chains."

Grinning, she ignored his exaggerated leer. "The

question now is whether we take the next step slow, or jump on a plane and zip out to Vegas before returning to our separate duty stations. Personally, I vote for Vegas.''

Just like that, Mac felt the worry and frustration and disgust at his lack of control over his life slide out of him. She was so sure, so certain. Her brown eyes held not the faintest trace of doubt.

He knew then that it didn't matter what the medical evaluation board decided. The corps had filled his mind and his heart all these years. He suspected both would be now fully occupied by Lieutenant Caroline Dunn.

Before he could tell her so, a ferocious pounding rattled the door in the other room.

''Oh, no!'' Cari groaned. ''Why does this always happen when we get naked?''

''You stay naked. I'll get it this time.''

Shaking his uniform pants, he stepped into them and dragged them on. Cari reached across the bed to keep them up around his hips while he worked the zipper.

''Thanks.'' His flashed her a quick grin. ''We make a heck of a team, Dunn.''

''So we do,'' she returned smugly.

Still grinning, Mac left her amid the tumbled covers and closed the bedroom doors. He opened the one in the living room to find Jill Bradshaw in the hall, her fist raised to pound again. The cop's startled glance zeroed in on his bare chest, dropped to his shoeless feet and whipped up to his amused face.

"Sorry to interrupt," she said got out after a moment. "If Cari's in there with you, she might want to turn on the television."

The sound of her former roommate's voice brought Cari's head popping through the crack in the bedroom door.

"Why? What's up?"

"A news flash just came on. Evidently a cruise ship out of Galveston lost one of its stabilizers. The storm's tossing the liner around like a toy boat."

"Oh, Lord!" Dragging the sheet she'd wrapped around her, Cari made for the TV. "Anyone want to bet two thousand passengers are upchucking all over that ship right now?"

Neither Mac nor Jill took her up on the bet, which was smart, as the news chopper's aerial shot of the floundering ship made even Cari's stomach turn queasy. The helicopter's high-powered spots barely cut through the sheets of rain and winds that sent walls of angry water smashing across the vessel's bow.

"She's floundering," Cari muttered, her gaze narrowed on the screen. "They'd better start taking off her passengers, like fast."

As if to confirm her assessment of the situation, the

newscaster pitched his voice over the howling winds to advise that the coast guard had ordered them to vacate the area immediately so as not to interfere with rescue operations. White knuckled, Cari clutched the sheet.

"The coast guard units here and at Kingsville will respond," she told the others. "Navy rescue craft, as well. They'll have to shuttle the passengers in by shifts. The operation will take all night."

Dropping into the chair at the desk, she reached for the phone and asked the operator to connect her to the coast guard operations center. She wasn't surprised when the on-duty controller ascertained she wasn't reporting an emergency then put her on hold for a good five minutes. When he came back on, Cari cut right to the purpose of her call.

"This is Lieutenant Caroline Dunn, United States Coast Guard. I'm on detached duty here at Corpus Christi. Tell your C.O. I'm available if he needs more hands to assist in the rescue operation."

"Will do, ma'am. Give me your number and I'll pass it to the skipper."

After that, there was nothing to do but watch as the local rescue units battled nature's fury. Cari and Mac retreated to the bedroom only long enough to dress. Two hours crawled by, long stretches filled with tossing seas and a steady progression of rescue craft pinned in the unrelenting glare of the aircraft circling overhead. Jill rapped on the door again, this time with Cody, Kate and Dave in tow.

Her face grim, Kate delivered more bad news. "I just checked the weather service computers. We've got another front moving down from the north. The two are going to collide right over this corner of the Gulf. The situation is going to get a whole lot worse before it gets better."

Her prediction was right on target. Where the seas were angry before, they soon turned vicious. The news agencies reported forty- and fifty-foot swells. Shots of the cruise ship showed the liner battered by white-capped swells that leaped and crashed around it like furies.

Cari was huddled in front of the TV with the rest of the Pegasus team when the phone rang. Thinking it was the coast guard controller, she snatched up the receiver.

"Lieutenant Dunn."

"Cari!" Her sister's frantic voice jumped across the line. "Is Paulo there with you?"

Her fist went tight on the phone. "No, he's not."

"We can't find him. We think he's run away."

"Why, for God's sake?"

"Jack found him playing with a rusty old pocket-knife. He was afraid one of the other kids might cut themselves and tried to take it away."

"Oh, no!"

She'd forgotten all about the boy's prize possession! She should have warned Deb he had it, explained how much it meant to him.

"How long has he been missing?"

Mac pushed out of his chair and came across the room. "How long has who been missing?"

"Paulo."

She angled the receiver so he could listen to Deb's rushed account.

"Paulo agreed to give Jack the knife. I thought he understood we were only holding it for safekeeping, but when we went up to check on the kids, he was gone. So was the knife."

"Have you called the Whites?"

"I checked with them first."

Mac snatched the phone out of Cari's hand. "What about the hospital? He might have gone there looking for me."

"I already called there. No one's seen him. Jack went out to search up and down the beach." Her voice wavered, cracked. "Oh, Mac, I hate to think Paulo might be wandering around in this storm."

Chapter 14

After instructing Deb to notify the police about Paulo's disappearance, Cari, Mac and the rest of the Pegasus cadre raced through the sheeting rain to the Hamiltons' beachside condo. The Whites arrived mere minutes later, as did a team of police officers and a hastily assembled group of local volunteers.

While Deb manned a mini-command post set up in the kitchen, searchers combed an area stretching from the populated sectors in the north to the Padre Island national seashore farther south. The searchers stayed out until well past midnight. Buffeted by wind, lashed by rain, they went door to door in the developed areas and used ATVs to comb the dunes.

The police called a halt to the official search just after 1:00 a.m. and asked the volunteers to reassemble come daylight. Mac, Cari, Jack, the Whites and the rest of the Pegasus crew gathered at the condo to regroup. Downing mugs of steaming coffee, they prepared to go back out again. A thoroughly miserable Jack shoved back the hood of his canary-yellow rain jacket and dragged a hand over his face.

"I feel lousy about that business with the knife. I didn't have any idea it meant so much to Paulo."

"That was our fault," Janice White said wearily. She was as soaked as the rest of them. Water dripped from her lashes and her strawberry-blond hair stood up in wet spikes. "We should have explained how careful Paulo always was with it around the other children. I'm surprised he ran away because you took it, though. The first few times Harry confiscated it, Paulo just rooted around the mission until he found it again."

Jack took small comfort from her words. Mac understood how he felt. He'd sensed something was troubling the kid, had tried to ferret it out of him. The best he'd been able to do was offer hearty assurances he'd be there when and if Paulo went into surgery.

A kid needed more than assurances. From bitter experience, Mac knew they needed a hand to hang on to. One that wouldn't let go through the rough times or the good.

"I'm going back out," he said abruptly.

He returned his mug to the kitchen counter with a thud, slopping hot coffee onto the back of his hand. He ignored the sting and dragged up the hood of his borrowed squall jacket. His uniform pants were drenched from the knees down and his shoes would never take another shine, but a lack of military precision didn't concern him at the moment.

Cari edged around the counter. Her hand caught his and made soothing little circles on the still-stinging skin.

"We'll find him," she said softly.

She'd guessed his guilt, his gut-wrenching sense of having failed Paulo as so many adults had failed Mac during his younger, wilder years. Despite the worry darkening her eyes, she was taking time to let him know she understood.

Funny, he'd never talked about his past. Had never needed to talk about it. Cari was the only one he could remember opening up to, and then with little more than the sketchiest details. Yet the bits he'd shared with her had given her a clearer insight into his thinking than he'd realized. For the first time, Mac had an inkling of what it would be like to share his life, his bed, even his thoughts with someone.

No, not *someone*.

With Cari.

Turning his palm up, he gave her fingers a tight, reassuring squeeze. "Damn straight, we'll find him."

He was halfway to the door when the shrill of the phone froze him in his tracks. Everyone in the kitchen jerked toward the wall-mounted unit. Leaping out of his seat with a look of anxious hope, Jack reached across the counter and snatched up the receiver.

"Hamilton here."

A moment later his shoulders drooped in disappointment. Turning, he held the phone out to his sister-in-law.

"It's the coast guard operations center."

"Oh, hell," Cari muttered. Her wet sneakers squishing on the tile, she crossed the kitchen. "I forgot about that cruise ship. God, I hope it hasn't gone down."

For several tense moments, it looked to the others in the kitchen that the worst had indeed happened. Cari identified herself, listened to the controller for a few seconds and suddenly stiffened.

"How far out are they?"

Her knuckles turned bone-white where she clutched the phone. Every vestige of color drained from her face. Her glance cut to Mac to her sister and back again.

His insides went cold. The call was about Paulo. He could see it in her face.

"Advise the RCC I'm on my way."

Slamming the phone into its cradle, she faced the tense, silent group.

"The coast guard Rescue Coordination Center just received a distress call from the captain of a commercial fishing boat. The *Aransas Star* put out from the docks just north of here earlier this evening, intending to edge around the worst of the storm so its crew could set their tuna lines come dawn. The boat had almost cleared the storm area when the second front hit. Its engine took a horrific beating fighting those swells and seized."

"Seized?" Deb gasped. "Like in *died?*"

"Like in *died.* When the crew went down to try to restart the engine they discovered a stowaway. He won't tell them his name…"

"Because he can't," Mac guessed grimly.

White-lipped, Cari nodded. "Their description of the boy tallies. It's Paulo."

The questions flew at her then, fast and furious.

"Did they get the engine restarted?"

"Are they bringing Paulo in?"

"Is the coast guard going after them?"

She shook her head. "No to the first two. As for the third, the Rescue Coordination Center is looking to see what assets they can redirect from the crippled cruise ship. Hopefully, they'll have a chopper or a cutter on the way by the time we get there."

"We're wasting time here," Mac snapped. "Let's go."

Deb and Jack stayed with their kids. The Whites remained at the condo as well, since their civilian status wouldn't allow them access to the restricted RCC. The six Pegasus team members piled into their vehicles and tailed Cari back to the naval air station.

The Rescue Coordination Center was like a dozen others Cari had pulled duty in. A wall-sized screen displayed a huge, computerized map of the Gulf. Controllers sat at a U-shaped console that gave them an unobstructed view of the screen while they synthesized the information pouring in by phone, fax, radio and computer. Given the level of activity, the very air inside the center vibrated with tension.

Cari pinpointed the location of the cruise ship with a single glance at the screen. The flashing red icon representing the ship looked like a giant queen bee, surrounded by hoards of rescue craft that buzzed around her like drones. Several pleasure boats were in distress as well, Cari saw. And there, in the northeast corner of the operational sector, was the flashing signal marking the position of the *Aransas Star*.

The center's commanding officer dragged his attention from the screen only long enough to brief the new arrivals. Mac was the only one of the group wearing a uniform, but the C.O. recognized Cari instantly. The coast guard was a relatively small service and most of the officers had crossed paths at one time or another.

Swiftly, Cari introduced the others. The C.O. accepted Jill's army status, Doc Richardson's Public Health Service background and Dave Scott's air force experience without a blink. His interest quickened when he learned Kate Hargrave was one of the National Oceanic and Atmospheric Administration's famed hurricane hunters. The National Weather Service was one of NOAA's major sub-units and, it turned out, had accurately predicted the turbulence that would occur when the second front moved in and collided with the first.

"We managed to get a warning out to most of the ships at sea," the rescue coordinator said, brushing a hand through his short, sandy hair. "If the cruise liner hadn't lost a stabilizer, she would have made port before the second front hit."

"How's the off-load of passengers progressing?" Cari asked.

"More slowly than we'd like. We've pressed all available navy, coast guard and customs service vessels into service, along with choppers from every base along the Gulf. But with these winds and swells, it's hell trying to bring the rescue craft alongside the liner."

"What about the fishing boat? We think the stowaway they found aboard is the same child we reported missing some hours ago.''

His face etched with sharp creases, the commander eyed the flashing red icon in the northeast sector of his operations area. ''They're more than a hundred nautical miles out. I'm diverting a chopper but will have to refuel it in flight. We're requesting a tanker orbit now.''

Cari's stomach sank. Bellying the rescue chopper up to a tanker in these winds would eat a precious thirty minutes. Sending it across a hundred nautical miles of storm-tossed sea would eat at least another hour. The fishing boat couldn't take another hour and a half of being pounded by these murderous swells.

Mac did the math as swiftly as Cari did, but grabbed on to a different solution.

''We've got our own craft,'' he informed the commander brusquely. ''It's got twice the air speed of a chopper. What's more, it's fueled and ready to fly.''

Cari whipped around. ''*Pegasus* isn't configured for deep-water rescue.''

''It's equipped with a Survivor Retrieval System,'' Kate reminded her. ''We used it to haul Mac out of the river.''

''The SRS won't hack it in these kinds of seas. We'd need a harness sling or a basket.''

She spun around again, an urgent question on her face. Her coast guard comrade answered with a quick nod. "We can supply a sling, but the baskets are all in use."

His pronouncement galvanized the entire Pegasus cadre. Dave Scott jumped in with confirmation that he'd prepped the craft for departure and had it ready to fly. Kate added that she could program in the current weather patterns en route and take them around the worst of the storm. Jill, ever conscious of her responsibilities as chief of security for *Pegasus*, issued a quick caution.

"We're talking about flying a multimillion-dollar prototype vehicle into howling, gale-force winds. We should obtain Captain Westfall's concurrence before we put the vehicle at risk."

"Get him on a secure line," Mac bit out. "Now!"

They tracked him to his hotel in Washington. Jill's call dragged Captain Westfall from a sound sleep. Succinctly, she explained the situation and requested his concurrence to include *Pegasus* as part of the multiservice rescue operation. She flipped her cell phone shut a few moments later with a tight, satisfied smile.

"He says to get our butts in gear and *Pegasus* in the air."

Cari's admiration for the lean, taciturn naval officer kicked up another notch. He shouldered overall responsibility for the Pegasus project, had invested months of his life and countless hours of sleep attempting to shake the last of the bugs out of the prototype. Yet he didn't hesitate to give them the green light and send his baby into harm's way once more.

"Okay, people," Mac snapped. "Let's move it."

After a fast detour to their on-base quarters to retrieve their gear and scramble into uniforms, the team raced to the hangar the navy had turned over to house *Pegasus* until its flight home. Dave had called ahead to the ground crew. The crew had *Pegasus* prepped and preflighted when the team arrived at the hangar. Moments later, a coast guard truck came screeching up with a harness sling.

Every member of the crew donned inflatable life vests and climbed aboard. Kate settled into the cockpit beside Dave and maintained a direct link to the National Weather Service throughout the turbulent flight. As promised, she directed the pilot around the worst of the storm, but even on the perimeter the winds were still so strong they whipped the craft around in the sky.

Forty stomach-twisting minutes later, Dave got a radar lock on the fishing boat. Struggling with the controls, he throttled back, tilted the engines and took *Pegasus* from forward flight to hover mode. Instead of flying into the winds, the craft was now at their mercy. They slammed *Pegasus* from what seemed like a dozen different directions at once. Sweating, straining, Dave fought to keep the wildly bucking craft in position over the boat. Everyone aboard held their breath until he raised the boat's captain on an emergency frequency.

"They see our lights," he informed those in the rear, shouting into his mike to be heard above the screaming winds. "The captain says we got here just in time. They're taking on water, fast."

"What about Paulo?" Mac yelled into the mike. "Is he okay?"

"Roger that. I'm going to raise the hatch. Make sure all lifelines are secure."

They took the warning seriously. Without the harnesses securing them to lines hooked into ringbolts in the bulkhead, they might well be sucked out into the maelstrom. Mac got a thumbs-up from the other three and confirmed their ready status.

"All secure!"

When the side hatch slid up, hell poured in. Rain lashed through the rear compartment. Wind ricocheted off the bulkheads and slammed into every immoveable object. *Pegasus* bucked wildly again, gyrating through the sky while Dave fought to compensate for the now gaping hole in the side of his craft.

For a few terrifying seconds, Cari's worst nightmare came back to haunt her. Only this time they weren't skimming along a green river with an enemy patrol boat on their tails. This time, they were suspended above a crashing sea, tossed around like a toy by nature's most malevolent forces.

The stomach-twisting fear was the same, though, as was the desperate realization that the odds were against them. She allowed herself one throat-closing glimpse through the hatch at the boat wallowing in the vicious seas below. There was one instant of liquid panic before she spotted the crew scattered across the deck, clinging desperately to lifelines.

Then her mind snapped into focus. Eyes narrowed to slits against the stinging rain, she searched the deck until she spotted a small figure huddled against the forward bulkhead. Like the others, Paulo was bundled into a bulky life jacket and tethered to a lifeline to keep from being swept overboard.

Her heart lurched, but she forced back her suffocating fear for the boy and reminded herself she was an officer in the U.S. Coast Guard. Years of command kicked in. Training and experience took over. Her gloved hand went to the lever that operated the Survivor Retrieval System.

"I'm activating the SRS," she bellowed into the mike. "Advise the crew of the *Star* to watch for the lead and try to hook it in."

While Cari extracted the firing tube and primed it, Jill and Doc checked to make sure the weighted lead was securely attached to the lightweight but almost indestructible nylon rope.

"Stand clear!"

The other two scrambled back. Cari braced herself as best she could in the open hatch. Rain slashed at her face. Wind whipped her hair into her eyes. Eyes narrowed to slits, arms extended, heart pounding, she aimed at a patch of boiling sea beyond the bow of the boat.

The weighted lead exploded out of the tube and shot through the air. For a wild, joyous moment, Cari thought she'd calculated the force and direction of the winds exactly right.

What she couldn't factor into her calculations was the capriciousness of the storm. The lead was still sailing through the swirling gray clouds when the wind suddenly shifted. A blast came out of the west, knocked *Pegasus* sideways and would have tossed everyone in the rear compartment onto their butts if not for their lifelines. When Cari got her feet under her again, she saw the lead had hit well aft of the boat.

With a vicious curse, she slammed the system into Reverse and reeled the lead back in. While she loaded another cartridge into the firing tube, Mac went down on one knee and coiled the wet, snaking rope to keep it from tangling when it shot out again.

It took four desperate tries to land the line within a few yards of the *Aransas Star*. Almost sobbing with relief, Cari watched the life-jacketed figures aboard the boat hook the line and drag it in.

It took only a few seconds to attach the rope to the flexible steel cable wound around the winch, a few more to make sure the rescue sling was securely attached to the cable. Once that was done, Cari hit the switch to deploy the hoist.

The moveable arm swung out. Another flick of the switch released the winch. Its gears sang as cable played out and the rescue sling plunged downward. Below, the crew of the *Star* frantically hauled on the nylon lead rope to guide the sling onto the deck.

As much as she wanted to take Paulo off first, Cari knew he needed to see how the hoist worked, had to understand that he should keep his arms locked to his side and the harness tight around his chest.

"Tell them to send up one of the crew first," Cari shouted to Dave via the intercom.

He didn't question her decision. The radio crackled with static as he relayed the order. Almost blinded by the sheeting rain, Cari hung on to her lifeline and leaned out of the hatch to watch while one of the crewmen scrambled into the harness.

He was still yanking on the chest straps when the *Star* plunged into a trough and the deck dropped out from under him. He dangled like a puppet above the boat, spinning in the wind.

Cari shoved the SRS into Reverse and brought him

up. When he was level with the hatch, she swung the retrieval arm in. Doc caught the man's arm, Jill one of his legs. The moment they had him free of the sling, Cari swung the arm out again.

Her heart jumped into her throat when she looked down and saw the *Aransas Star*'s decks were almost completely awash. The crashing waves had knocked the slicker-clad figures off their feet. They whipped back and forth through the frothing water at the ends of their lifelines, as helpless as the tuna they hooked on their fishing lines. Cari didn't breathe until she spotted Paulo among the frothing water. Praying the boy understood what he had to do, she shouted into her mike.

"Tell them to send Paulo up next!"

"Roger."

Mac shortened his lifeline and fought the winds at the open hatch. His jaw clenched so tight the bones ground together. He'd served two combat tours, first in Afghanistan, then in Iraq. He'd seen men go down, had heard their screams as bullets ripped into them. The icy, controlled terror of combat didn't compare to the fear that ripped into him now.

Paulo was so small, so thin. If he lifted his arms, if he wiggled or twisted too much, he could slip right out of that harness.

Mac knew Cari had already considered and discarded the only other option—having one of the other crewmen strap himself in and bring the boy up with him. The savage wind could tear the kid right out of the man's arms.

Mac's heart hammered as two crewmen staggered across the deck toward the boy. They dragged him to his feet. Buckled on the harness. Unhooked his life-line. Waved to the wildly gyrating craft.

"Hang on, kid. Hang on. Hang on."

Mac repeated the low, fierce litany with every turn of the winch. He could see the boy rise foot by foot. His dark hair was plastered to his skull, his face chalk-white above his orange life vest.

Cari's gloved fist hovered over the switch that would swing the retrieval arm inward. Mac was just letting himself believe they'd get the boy aboard when a brutal downdraft slammed into *Pegasus.* The craft nosedived, spiraling straight down. The steep drop knocked Jill and Cari off balance. Doc threw himself over the rescued crewman to keep him from crashing into the forward bulkhead. Mac stayed up-right by sheer force of will and an iron grip on his lifeline.

His heart stopping, he saw the waves reach up and swallow the small figure at the end of the cable. Paulo went under, popped up and was dragged through one crashing wall of water after another.

Dave brought the nose up mere seconds later, but before he could regain altitude another wave smashed into Paulo. When the towering wave rolled past, the harness was empty.

Mac didn't hesitate, didn't give his injured shoulder so much as a single thought. Whipping down his good arm, he unsnapped his lifeline.

A heartbeat later he plunged into the sea.

Chapter 15

Mac sank into a deep trough. He'd no sooner hit than a towering, eighty-foot wave smashed down on top of him. The brutal force drove him downward. So hard, the violence sucked a boot right off his foot. So deep, he couldn't tell top from bottom. So far, his lungs were bursting by the time the vicious wave rolled past and his life jacket brought him popping to the surface.

The massive swells batted at him, battered him, tossed him from side to side. Gritting his teeth, Mac kicked and twisted and rode the violent swells until he spotted Paulo's orange life vest not ten yards away. The steel cable dragged the water just beyond him.

Mac twisted onto his side and buried his bad shoulder in the water. Scissor-kicking, he used his good arm to battle through the swells.

"Paulo!"

The wind flung his shout back in his face. With it came a mouth full of salt water. Spitting, cursing, kicking with every ounce of strength he possessed, Mac cut through the last few yards and got a fist on the back of the boy's vest.

Frantic, Paulo squirmed around and grabbed his rescuer with both hands just above the biceps. As the force of the sea tried to separate them, he clung desperately to Mac's bad arm. Agony knifed through him. The white-capped waves and raging sea blurred. The pain paralyzed him. For an instant, maybe two, his mind and body froze. Teeth grinding, he forced back the black haze.

"Put your arms around my neck."

He had to shout the instruction in the boy's ear to be heard over the snarl of wind and sea.

"Paulo! Climb up and wrap your arms around my neck!"

His dark eyes dilated with terror, the boy crawled up Mac's chest and locked his arms.

"Now kick," Mac yelled. "Kick hard!"

Sandwiched together by the brutal force of the waves, they fought their way to the cable.

Cari watched the life-and-death struggle from

above. Every stroke was a desperate prayer, every pulverizing wave stabbed her agonizing hope in the heart. On the far side of the hatch Cody and Jill stood ready to unhook their lifelines and jump in. If Mac and Paulo went under once more, just once, one of them would hit the water. All the while, Dave sweated and strained to keep *Pegasus* in a hover.

"A few more feet," Cari muttered, her throat raw. "Just a few feet."

She had to time this exactly right. Her hand trembled over the switch while Mac rode the crest of a wave toward the cable. When he was a body length away, Cari hit Reverse. The winch whirred, the cable retracted, and the harness sling rose from the angry green depths. As soon as it broke the surface, she slammed her fist on the switch to halt the winch.

The harness sling dangled just feet from Mac's face. Calling on reserves he wasn't sure he had, he jackknifed his body and propelled forward. He thrust his good arm through the sling, wrestled it over his head, but wasn't about to let Paulo loosen his death grip so he could shimmy the rest of his body into it and attempt to buckle the harness one-handed. Locking the boy against his chest with his good arm, he jerked his head back.

"Bring us up!"

His hoarse bellow got lost in the wind, but Cari

was watching and waiting for his signal. Mac saw the cable go taut, felt the sling dig into his armpit.

When they cleared the roiling surface, the wind set them twisting and swinging like a pendulum. The sea leaped up, crashed around them, tried to devour them yet again. With a whimper of sheer terror, Paulo buried his face in Mac's neck.

The boy's weight dragged at him. The sling felt as though it was slicing him in half. His shoulder was a fireball of pain. Mac blanked his mind to everything but the need to keep his good arm locked around the kid.

Then they cleared the hatch, Cari swung the hoist arm in and anxious hands reached out.

''We've got him,'' Cody shouted. ''Mac, we've got him. Let go!''

An exhausting hour and a half later, *Pegasus* swooped down on the naval air station's rain-drenched runway. A watery dawn was graying the sky to the east as the endless, storm-wracked night slowly gave way to day.

The ground crew was waiting to recover the craft. While Dave went through the shut-down procedures, Kate, Doc and Jill delivered the crew of the *Aransas Star* to the Rescue Coordination Center to make the necessary notifications. Cari and Mac took Paulo back to the condo where the Hamiltons and the Whites waited.

The storm had left its mark. The slowly gathering dawn revealed uprooted palm trees and scattered debris en route to the beachside vacation rentals, but the condos themselves sustained no storm damage. Light poured through the downstairs windows of the unit Cari had rented for her sister. The kids were still asleep, she guessed, but the adults had all spent a long, tension-racked night.

She pulled into the parking space and killed the vehicle's engine. A quick glimpse in the rearview mirror showed eyes hollowed by fatigue and a face framed by the wild, wind-whipped tangles that had escaped her hair clip. Her wet uniform felt clammy in the cool October dawn. Her entire body ached from the strain and tension of the long night.

Her passengers weren't in much better shape. Paulo climbed out of the vehicle and hunched his thin shoulders under the blanket they'd draped around him aboard *Pegasus*. His face was pinched and white and scared. Cari knew he expected a scolding. Or worse.

Mac looked every bit as battered by the elements as the boy. His uniform hung in wet folds. Fatigue had carved deep grooves in his face. His plunge into the sea had left him carrying his shoulder stiffly. *Very* stiffly. Still, he managed to hunker down on one knee when Paulo balked at going into the house.

"Time to face the music, kid." He softened the gruff admonishment by knuckling the boy's head. "You need to tell the Whites and the Hamiltons you're sorry for scaring them the way you did."

He also needed to explain why he'd run away. Neither Cari nor Mac had pressed the shivering, frightened boy for answers, but they both suspected something other than a hassle over his pocketknife had driven Paulo out into the storm.

The others firmly seconded their opinion that explanations could come later. After startling the boy with a fierce hug, Deb waited only until Janice White had translated Paulo's assurances that he was all right to whisk him upstairs for a hot shower and dry clothes. Jack used their absence to supply Cari and Mac with coffee and cook up a huge batch of bacon, scrambled eggs and refrigerator biscuits. All the while, he and the Whites pumped them for details about the rescue at sea.

Deb brought Paulo back downstairs twenty minutes later. After getting the nod from Reverend White, the boy attacked his plate of eggs and bacon like a starving wolf pup. While he gulped down the hot food and glass after glass of milk, Cari and Mac gave Deb an abbreviated version of the saga they'd just related to the others.

Finally it was Paulo's turn. He set down his milk glass and tried for his habitual scowl, but Mac cut him off at the pass. "What did we talk about outside, kid?"

Pushing out his lower lip, Paulo brought up his hands. Janice White interpreted.

"He says he's sorry for frightening us."

Jack leaned forward. His voice heavy with regret, he offered an apology of his own. "I'm sorry, too, Paulo. I didn't understand how important that pocketknife is to you. I wasn't going to keep it or throw it away, just put it somewhere safe."

The boy's dark eyes held only misery as he signed a response.

"It doesn't matter about the knife," Janice translated. "It's at the bottom of the ocean, anyway."

"Oh, no!" Cari clucked sympathetically. "Was it in your pocket when you went into sea?"

His nod confirmed her guess. Slowly, reluctantly, his hands shaped more phrases.

"He says he's wants to go back to Caribe. He can survive alone in the jungle. He's done it before. That way he won't be such trouble to everyone."

"You're not trouble!" Deb protested, her mother's heart shredding at the idea of a child alone in a jungle. "No trouble at all."

Paulo turned to her and Jack, pleading for understanding with his hands and his face.

"He says you have burden enough with your family. He knows you only took him in because the other family, the one who'd said they would adopt him, didn't want him. He thought maybe…"

The small hands went still.

"What?" Janice prompted after a moment. "What did you think, Paulo?"

The boy shot a look comprised of equal parts guilt and unhappiness at the two figures in uniform.

"He thought maybe Major Mac or the lieutenant would take him. He would have been a good son. Very quiet. Work very hard."

Cari's throat closed. "We would have taken you if we could, Paulo."

"He knows you could not," Janice translated. "He understands the major must go to the hospital for a long time. And he heard you explain to your sister that you go away on ships."

Oh, God! *That's* why he'd run away. He'd heard her talking to Deb yesterday afternoon. The realization settled with sickening certainty in Cari's stomach.

She tried to recall her exact words, then realized they didn't matter. What mattered was that she'd shattered his secret hope that she or Mac would give him a home.

She couldn't tell him that she'd harbored the same secret hope. Or that hard, cold reality had forced her to abandon the idea before it could even take shape. As miserable as Paulo now, she reached across the table and curled her hand around his.

"Now it's my turn to apologize. I'm sorry if it sounded as though I didn't want you. I do. I'd give you a home in a heartbeat if I could. So would Major Mac."

She looked to Mac, expecting him to jump right in with a vigorous second. His hesitation surprised her almost as much as the sudden narrowing of his eyes when they met hers. The face he turned to Paulo a moment later, though, showed only honest sincerity.

"She's telling you the truth. Either one of us would be proud to call you son."

Once more he hesitated, choosing his words carefully so as not to offer false hope.

"Stay with Mr. and Mrs. Hamilton, kid. See how things shake out. If you still want to go back to Caribe a few months or a year from now, I'll take you myself and make sure you have a home other than the jungle. Deal?"

No one at the table needed an interpretation of

Paulo's response. Cupping his hand, he moved it slowly up and down much like a head nodding a reluctant agreement.

Mac was quiet during the short drive back to the visiting officers' quarters. Cari, too, had little to say. Weariness, guilt and a sharp, stinging regret had taken the edge off her adrenaline high from plucking Paulo and the crew of the *Star* from the sea. Not until she and Mac had showered and changed into dry clothes did she add a healthy dose of anger to her mix of emotions.

Mac sparked it when she walked into the living room after her shower, still toweling her wet hair. His glance was cool as it skimmed over her cotton sweater and slacks before settling on her face.

Cari's hands stilled. She cocked her head, trying to assess his expression. "That's the second time you've looked at me like that," she commented.

"Like how?"

"Like you blame me for the fact that Paulo almost drowned."

"What?"

Draping the fluffy yellow towel around her neck, she raked a hand through her damp hair. "You can't blame me any more than I blame myself. I hate that Paulo overheard Deb and me. You have to know I never intended to…"

"Don't be stupid. No one blames you, least of all me."

His curt tone brought her chin up. "Then why the hell are you so uptight?"

Irritation pushed through her guilt and regret. After all they'd gone through together, the man could show some consideration here. Maybe even take her in his arms.

He did neither. If anything, his expression went more glacial. "You don't know?"

"Obviously not," she snapped, "or I wouldn't have asked."

Mac crossed the room in three swift strides. Even in shorts and the flip-flops he'd brought with him, the man could be intimidating. Cari stood her ground but didn't particularly care for the dangerous glint in his hazel eyes.

"Just tell me one thing," he growled. "Last night, when we were in bed, why did you toss out the idea of jumping a plane for a quick trip to Vegas?"

The abrupt change in direction confused her. Her fists tight on the ends of the towel, she fired back in the same belligerent tone.

"Because you said you love me and I said ditto. People *do* sometimes get married when they discover they're in love."

"Or when they want to adopt a kid."

Cari reared back. "You... You think I suggested Vegas because I wanted to give Paulo a home?"

Mac's face was relentless above his sling. "Isn't that why you broke things off with Jerry-boy? Because you wanted children and he didn't?"

Her mouth opened. Clamped shut. After a seething moment, she admitted the brutal truth.

"That was part of it."

Mac hooked a brow. "Only part?"

"Okay, that was the main reason. The fact that I was lusting after a certain hardheaded marine might have had something to do with it, too."

When Mac maintained his politely disbelieving expression, Cari blew out a long breath and forced herself to let go of her anger. The need to make him understand was too important, too urgent for sarcasm or sharp retorts.

"What I feel for you has nothing to do with Jerry or Paulo or my desire to have children. I love you. I want to spend the rest of my life with you." Sighing, she reached up to curve a palm over his cheek. "You'll just have to trust me on this, McIver."

To her infinite relief, he turned his head and pressed a kiss into her palm. The icy remoteness was gone when he faced her again, replaced by the first glimmer of a smile.

"You'll have to trust me, too."

"I will. I do."

"Even when I tell you I've decided to leave the corps to become a stay-at-home dad?"

Dumbstruck, Cari gaped up at him. Her hand slipped downward, hit his chest with a thump.

"What!"

His smile slipped into a rueful grin. Reaching up with his good arm, he covered her hand with his.

"I won't be much use to the corps with this shoulder, but I figure I can give Paulo adequate guidance and supervision."

She'd known it! Sensed right almost from the day her all-or-nothing, you're-in-or-you're-out marine took that bullet he would never settle for a career of restricted duty.

Part of her ached for him. The rest of her accepted that the decision was his to make—and knew without a moment's doubt he'd apply the same one hundred percent effort to loving her and Paulo.

Still, she had to ask. "Are you sure, Mac? I know how much the corps means to you."

"It'll always be part of me. You know the old saying. Once a marine, always a marine."

His palm flattened over hers. She could feel the strong, steady beat of his heart under his shirt. The smile in his eyes was just as steady and sure.

"You mean more, Cari. So much, much more. You

and Paulo and any other kids we might have if we try real hard and just happen to get lucky.''

He was handing her her dream, a family she could share the good and the bad times with. Children she could cuddle and spoil and watch grow. A man she could love with all that was in her.

Her heart singing, she went up on tiptoe and brushed his mouth with hers. ''I vote we get started on the trying real hard part right now.''

Epilogue

The ceremony kicked off with the ruffles and flourishes appropriate to a four-star general. Flanked by Captain Westfall, the vice chairman of the Joint Chiefs marched into a spotless hangar illuminated to almost painful intensity by the New Mexico sun. Although the January wind frisking through the wide-open hangar doors carried a definite nip, none of the officers who leaped to attention noticed its bite.

They stood at the head of the Pegasus cadre. Their service dress uniforms were knife-creased. Their ribbons, badges and accouterments glittered in the bright sunlight.

Jill Bradshaw in army-green with the crossed pistols of the Military Police Branch decorating her lapels.

Dave Scott wearing air force blue and rows of colorful ribbons topped by shiny silver wings.

Kate Hargrave in her navy blue skirt and jacket, with the shield of National Oceanic and Atmospheric Administration gleaming on her cap.

Cody Richardson, also in dark navy, wearing the anchor insignia of the U.S. Public Health Service.

Cari with shoulders squared and her gold wedding band gleaming in the afternoon sunlight.

Mac standing tall and proud in his dress blues for the last time.

Another ceremony would follow this one. After three months of intensive physical therapy, Major Russ McIver was being released from active duty and medically retired from the United States Marine Corps. The ceremony would be done by Captain Westfall—newly engaged to Dr. Janice White— immediately following the vice chairman's formal acceptance of the military's new attack/assault vehicle.

Pegasus gleamed white and sleek across the hangar. The vehicle would go into full production soon. Within a few short months, personnel from combat units stateside and abroad would enter training to learn how to maximize its unique abilities. Dave Scott was transferring to the designated training base in Georgia, just a few hours up the road from

Kate's base in Tampa. Cari had been selected for the training cadre, too.

She knew Captain Westfall had pulled some strings to make that assignment happen. It would give Mac time to transition to full civilian life, Paulo time to adjust to the artificial voice box doctors had implanted two weeks ago, and Cari to have three years of shore duty to enjoy motherhood.

Resisting the impulse to grin idiotically, she kept her back straight and her hand from straying to her belly in a protective gesture as old as time. The time for wonder and delight and celebration would come later, when she and Mac could share with their comrades in arms the results of the home pregnancy test she'd taken this morning.

Right now, her focus needed to remain on the ceremony marking the end of the operational test phase. *Pegasus* had proved himself—on land, air and sea. This was his moment in the sun, a moment every man and woman present took inestimable pride in.

When the general stepped to the podium to deliver the congratulations of the six service chiefs, the massed cadre went to parade rest. Legs spread. Hands whipped to the small of the back. Spines lost only a minimal degree of rigidity.

While the general adjusted his mike, a ripple of emotion passed through the officers. One by one they slipped a glance to the right, then to the left. The small smiles they gave each other reflected pride of accomplishment, along with the smug knowledge they shared that indefinable mix of adventurous heart and fearless spirit others called—for lack of a better term—the right stuff.

*   *   *   *   *

From *USA TODAY* bestselling author

MERLINE LOVELACE

TO PROTECT AND DEFEND

Trained to put their lives on the line.
Their hearts were another matter....

A Question of Intent
(Silhouette Intimate Moments #1255,
November 2003)

Full Throttle
(Silhouette Desire #1556, January 2004)

The Right Stuff
(Silhouette Intimate Moments #1279, March 2004)

Available at your favorite retail outlet.

Silhouette®
Where love comes alive™

INTIMATE MOMENTS®

#1285 COVER-UP—Ruth Langan

Devil's Cove

When bestselling novelist Jason Cooper returned to Devil's Cove and saw Emily Brennan again, the very scent of her perfume drew him irresistibly to his first love. But soon after his arrival, someone began threatening the beautiful doctor. Was it only a coincidence that the mysterious stalker bore a striking resemblance to the killer in Jason's latest book?

#1286 GUILTY SECRETS—Virginia Kantra

Cynical reporter Joe Reilly didn't believe in angels—human or otherwise. But the moment he was assigned to write an article on Nurse Nell Dolan, the "Angel of Ark Street," his reporter's instincts sprang to life. Nell's gut told her to keep her past—and her heart—under lock and key. Could he convince her to risk sharing her past secrets…in exchange for his love?

#1287 SHOCK WAVES—Jenna Mills

Psychic Brenna Scott sensed federal prosecutor Ethan Carrington was going to die…unless she could warn him in time. Ethan wasn't sure if her haunting visions were true—but the shock waves of desire he felt coursing through him were definitely genuine. Brenna felt the same intense connection to Ethan, but with a killer on their heels, she knew their future hinged on more than just destiny alone.

#1288 DANGEROUS ILLUSION—Melissa James

Agent Brendan McCall only had a few days to find and protect his former lover Elizabeth Silver. With an international killer gunning for her, Elizabeth was relieved when Brendan showed up and promised to keep her safe. His plan to protect her was simple: give her a new identity—with one stipulation. She had to agree to become his wife. Would this marriage of protection turn into a *real* union?

#1289 SHADOWS OF THE PAST—Frances Housden

A stalker had taught Maria Costello to trust no one, but when a gorgeous, rough-hewn stranger asked her for a date at the company's Christmas party, she broke all her rules and said yes to CEO Franc Jellic. His eyes promised her the one thing she'd denied herself: love. But would her newfound happiness with Franc trigger another deadly attack from her past?

#1290 HER PASSIONATE PROTECTOR—Laurey Bright

From the moment Sienna Rivers signed on to evaluate the artifacts found on a deep-sea expedition, she'd been running for her life from robbers, muggers…and from her feelings for her boss, Brodie Stanner. His carefree lifestyle brought back painful childhood memories of her father's philandering. But Brodie wasn't about to let Sienna slip through his fingers. Could he convince her that he was the one man who held the key to mend her heart?